"How are you?" Zach asked.

Kylie glanced up at him. "You mean, how am I doing since I caught my fiancé cheating on the day of my wedding, which I canceled at the last moment?"

Zach caught a smile before it could do more than curl one corner of his mouth. She had fire in her. He liked that about her. "Something like that."

She shrugged. "About like you'd expect, I guess. Mostly, I'm relieved that it happened the way it did and not in reverse order. If I'd have found out after the wedding, I'd be worse off. Sometimes, though, I wonder how much of it is my fault."

Zach gaped at her. "You can't be serious. This is not your fault. Any guy would be lucky to have you."

Sucking in a deep breath, he wrapped his palm around the cold glass of his beverage and measured his words. "You are well rid of Vincent."

* * *

Rocky Mountain Heirs:
When the greatest fortune of all is love.

Books by Arlene James

Love Inspired

*The Perfect Wedding
*An Old-Fashioned Love
*A Wife Worth Waiting For
*With Baby in Mind
The Heart's Voice
To Heal a Heart
Deck the Halls
A Family to Share
Butterfly Summer
A Love So Strong
When Love Comes Home
A Mommy in Mind
**His Small-Town Girl

**Her Small-Town Hero
**Their Small-Town Love
%Anna Meets Her Match
%A Match Made in Texas
A Mother's Gift
  "Dreaming of a Family"
%Baby Makes a Match
%An Unlikely Match
The Sheriff's Runaway Bride

*Everyday Miracles
**Eden, OK
%Chatam House

ARLENE JAMES

says, "Camp meetings, mission work and church attendance permeate my Oklahoma childhood memories. It was a golden time, which sustains me yet. However, only as a young widowed mother did I truly begin growing in my personal relationship with the Lord. Through adversity He has blessed me in countless ways, one of which is a second marriage so loving and romantic it still feels like courtship!"

After thirty-three years in Texas, Arlene James now resides in Bella Vista, Arkansas, with her beloved husband. Even after seventy-five novels, her need to write is greater than ever, a fact that frankly amazes her, as she's been at it since the eighth grade. She loves to hear from readers, and can be reached via her website at www.arlenejames.com.

The Sheriff's Runaway Bride

Arlene James

Love Inspired

Special thanks and acknowledgment to Arlene James for her participation in the Rocky Mountain Heirs miniseries

Recycling programs
for this product may
not exist in your area.

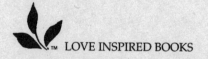

™ LOVE INSPIRED BOOKS

ISBN-13: 978-0-373-87686-0

THE SHERIFF'S RUNAWAY BRIDE

Copyright © 2011 by Harlequin Books S.A.

www.LoveInspiredBooks.com

Printed in U.S.A.

"Because of the oppression of the weak
and the groaning of the needy, I will now arise,"
says the LORD. "I will protect them
from those who malign them."
—*Psalms* 12:5

For my cousin, Terry Lynn Morris,
veteran, wounded warrior, retired peace officer and
so much more, definitely one of the "good guys."
With love,
DAR

Chapter One

"You're a long way from Miami, my friend," newly sworn Deputy Sheriff Zach Clayton muttered to himself, surveying the small, narrow office.

Disorganized and poorly arranged, with dust covering every conceivable surface, it hardly invited confidence. Apparently, his predecessor, Linden Diggers, hadn't filed anything in years. The best thing to do seemed to be to find some boxes in which to store all this detritus. He'd clean as he went along, then rearrange later.

Turning, Zach walked back through the door and past the white sedan bearing the logo and symbol of the county sheriff. The sheriff had promised that the rattletrap would be replaced "next year sometime."

Zach hadn't mentioned that he didn't intend to stay long enough to see that happen. He'd pass the year in Clayton, Colorado, as required by the terms of his grandfather George's will, but after that Zach would be ready to get back to his real life.

At least he prayed he'd be ready.

Plucking his mirrored sunshades from the chest pocket of his forest-green shirt with the Sheriff's Department insignia at the top of each sleeve, Zach slid the glasses onto his face and adjusted the brim of his forest-green ball cap. His khaki pants boasted wide green stripes that ran down the outside of each leg from his waist to the tops of his black western boots.

The uniform felt strange. He'd made detective his fourth year out of academy and had worn plain clothes ever since. Now here he stood in full regalia with a gun on his hip and a utility belt. He'd never expected to wear a uniform again, but then, he'd never expected to return to his hometown either.

From sheer habit, Zach took stock of his surroundings, surveying for activity in the immediate area. Swathed in bunting and American flags in honor of the upcoming Independence Day celebration, the downtown square seemed deserted, despite the two dozen or so cars in the small parking lot to the east of the familiar white clapboard church in the southwest corner of the greensward. Sweeping his gaze across the green, Zach saw that the gazebo, playground and picnic tables remained empty. Across the way, the parking spaces all stood empty in front of the pharmacy, the grocery, and the Cowboy Café diner. Even the Hair Today beauty parlor looked abandoned.

Zach turned his attention to Railroad Street, the town's main avenue, which ran east and west. A fat, red hen leisurely strolled beneath the only traffic light in town. Crossing Railroad, it wandered right down the middle of Eagle Street toward him. That meandering fowl seemed quintessential Clayton, Colorado. With a population around nine hundred, the whole town—which had been founded by his great-grandfather, Jim—wasn't much bigger than a good-size chicken coop and about as exciting.

Shaking his head, Zach moved past his black Jeep Wrangler, intending to snag a few boxes from the grocery. As he crossed the street, he caught movement from the corner of his eye. Halting, he turned his head just enough to get a full view. His brown eyebrows went up, arching over the gold rims of his sunshades, as he registered the sight before him.

A bride, white veil flowing out behind her, long skirt belling, ran toward him from the vicinity of the church, bouquet in hand. Zach dipped his chin and pushed down the dark glasses, peering over the rim, just to be certain that the altitude wasn't playing tricks with his sight.

Hot on her heels ran none other than his old nemesis and cousin, Vincent Clayton, dressed in a cheap black suit. Behind him trundled a stocky middle-aged fellow in a tuxedo. Instinctively, Zach strode forward just as Vincent caught up with the bride at the edge of the greensward. Zach didn't know what was going on, but he did know what a bully Vincent was, and the badge pinned to his shirt gave him all the authority he needed to intervene. Smiling grimly, he prepared to perform his first official act as deputy sheriff.

A beefy hand grabbed Kylie Jones's arm, yanking her to a stop.

"Dagnabit, Kylie, hold up!" Vincent bawled, hauling her around to face him.

"Let go!" For emphasis, the bride whacked him in the face with her bouquet, which he then tore from her hand and threw to the ground.

"It was just a kiss!" Vincent yelled, grappling with her.

"It was not!"

"Just a last kiss before I become a married man," he wheedled.

Yanking free, Kylie stumbled backward, then began edging closer to the uniformed officer who she'd spied coming out of Linden's old office only moments earlier. Everyone in town knew that they were getting a replacement to man the satellite office of the county sheriff's department now that Linden Diggers had retired, but no one had expected the new guy to show up on a Saturday morning. Conventional wisdom said he wouldn't make it to town until after the Fourth of July holiday. Thank God that had proved wrong!

Livid about her breaking their engagement just minutes before the wedding would have taken place, Vincent had tried to force her into the church. Spying the deputy, she had run instead. Now, with rescue just feet away, she stood her ground.

"Vincent, I heard you! The two of you were obviously together all night. And you were planning to meet her again next weekend!"

He turned on the charm…he was good at that. Pity he wasn't as good at telling the truth. "It was a joke, baby. That's all."

Vincent stood only a half foot taller than her own five-foot-three-inch frame, but he outweighed her by sixty or seventy pounds, all of it muscle. With his spiked blond hair, smooth, lantern jaw and bright blue eyes, he was a better than average-looking man, his features marred only slightly by a somewhat crooked nose. However, she'd been bothered for some time by a sense that Vincent was not all that he seemed, and now she had proof.

"I'm not an idiot, Vincent! I saw what the two of you were doing in that car, and I heard every word you said to her. What I don't understand is why you asked me to marry you if you want to be with *her!*"

He dropped all pretense of innocence, resorting to sneering justification instead. "I was just playing around, Kylie Jeanne. That's what men do. She might not be wife material, but at least she's fun. If you really want to know, she's a hot—"

Kylie slapped him smartly across the face, turning his head sharply to one side. For a long instant, the air seemed to sizzle with the sting of her hand. Then Vincent slowly brought his gaze around, his brow lowered in a thunderous expression of anger.

"You're going to regret that."

"Not as much as I'd regret marrying you!" she snapped, yanking up her skirt with both hands and whirling away.

Thankfully, the deputy had arrived on the scene and stood watching with the silent attention of a laser beam. Long-legged and slim-hipped, he looked to be at least a couple inches over six feet and packed enough upper-body weight to give even Vincent pause. Add the gun on his hip, and he became invincible. Kylie didn't waste an instant deciding to put him between her and her erstwhile fiancé. Zipping around the big man, she plastered herself to the deputy's back. That felt oddly right, not just safe but somehow fitting, almost familiar. She tilted her head, wondering how on earth that could be.

"Hold up!" Zach ordered, keenly aware of the slender, feminine form pressed against him.

Vincent halted in mid-stride, scowling, one palm cradling his reddened cheek.

The beauty of that slender, oval face with its luscious red lips and clear, moss-green eyes framed by very long, light-golden-brown curls had stunned Zach. At not much taller than five feet she was a slight thing, slender enough to hide completely behind him. The long-fingered hand grasping his arm displayed false, white-tipped fingernails, one of which had been torn loose by her assault on Vincent's cheek. Zach was not inclined to hold either the fake fingernails or the slap against her.

"Now, see here, Sheriff," Vincent said confidently, dropping his hand. "That's my fiancée, Kylie Jones." The name rang a bell in Zach's mind.

"Former fiancée!" she declared.

Vincent went on as if she hadn't even spoken. "I'm Vincent

Clayton. My great-granddaddy founded this town. This here
is just a case of wedding day jitters."

"This here," retorted Kylie Jeanne Jones, practically climbing Zach's back in order to speak over his shoulder, "is me
not making the worst mistake of my life by marrying you,
Vincent Clayton!"

"We'll just see what your daddy has to say about that!"
Vincent growled.

"Her daddy saw and heard you with that woman, too," said
the stout fellow, jogging up behind Vincent. He bent forward,
palms braced against his knees, and tried to catch his breath,
declaring, "No wedding! Not if my girl doesn't want it."

Vincent's face turned ugly. "Oh, yeah? We'll see about
that. My grandpa's not going to be happy about this, not one
bit, and you know what that means."

"Still throwing your weight around, huh, Vincent?" Zach
observed calmly, peeling off his shades.

Vincent did a double take, staggering back a single step,
before sneering, "Well, if it isn't Cousin Zach." He practically spat the name, scraping a scornful look from the insignia affixed to the front of Zach's cap to the rounded toes of
his black cowboy boots. "I should've known you'd crawl out
of that Miami swamp hole sooner or later."

"Looks like I made it just in time," Zach replied smoothly.

Vincent had put on weight, building up bulging muscles
in his chest and arms, but that didn't impress Zach one bit.
His own leaner form was not only adequately muscled but
well trained. He didn't doubt that he could take down Vincent in a fight, probably in three moves. He planned them in
his mind as Vincent gathered his nerve.

Jabbing a finger at him, Vincent scoffed, "This ain't like
old times, cuz, when your grandpa ruled the roost around
here. My daddy's mayor now, you know."

Zach did know. The sheriff had informed him at the

swearing-in that morning. Zach made the same comment now that he'd made then. "Good thing I'm on the county payroll, isn't it?"

"You just mind your own business," Vincent snarled.

"I am minding my business, *cuz*. A lawman can't walk away when he witnesses an assault."

"What assault?" Vincent demanded, holding out his hands as if to prove his innocence.

"Why, I do believe the lady slapped you. Turned your head right around."

Vincent's scowl cleared, replaced by slyness. "That's right. You saw it. She assaulted me. I could press charges, couldn't I?"

Behind him, Zach heard the feisty bride gasp. Her father straightened, a protest forming on his lips, but Zach quelled it with a single stern glance before settling his full attention on Vincent.

"You could. Now, if you want, I'll write up a report. You can look for it in Monday's papers."

"The papers!"

"New policy," Zach informed Vincent coolly. "All formal reports make the police blotters in all the county papers."

Knowing how little Vincent's grandfather, Samuel, liked having the public light shined on his business and his side of the family, Zach had suggested the policy himself just that morning after the county sheriff had so graciously performed a rare weekend swearing-in ceremony. The sheriff had readily agreed, and Zach considered that a fine accomplishment for his first day on the job. This was just icing on the cake.

He watched Vincent mull over his options and come to a decision. Finally, he shook his head. "Forget it."

"That's what I thought," Zach muttered.

Zach's grandfather, George Sr., hadn't been the most upstanding citizen, but at least he'd been blatant about his dealings. Samuel and his lot were sneaky, as Zach knew all too well.

Once, back in high school, Zach had been framed for stealing firewood—no small thing in cold country where many homes depended on the heat of a fireplace. A friend of Vincent's, Willy Bishop, had eventually confessed to being the culprit, but everyone knew Willy was a follower, not a leader, and none too bright. Zach could not prove that Vincent was behind the scheme, but the incident had given him firsthand knowledge of how that side of the family worked. It had also provided him with his dearest memory of his late grandfather. George Sr. had not been an easy or even likable man, but he'd never doubted Zach and had prevented his arrest until his innocence could be proved, keeping alive Zach's dream of making a career in law enforcement.

Later, of course, the old man had reverted to type and threatened to disown Zach when he'd refused to return home to Clayton after college. Though grateful for that early intervention, Zach would not have returned to Colorado just to please his grandfather, even if he'd known about the money. No one had ever dreamed that the old man was worth anything, let alone a fortune, not until the reading of the will a few weeks ago.

Even then, Zach might not have returned if things had been different in Miami and his youngest sister, Brooke, did not suspect Vincent of stirring up trouble for the family. She firmly believed that Vincent had kidnapped, or at least waylaid, her soon-to-be stepson, A.J., who was not yet three years old.

Thankfully, that situation had turned out well. Due to none other than Kylie Jones.

"Guess you'd best get on back to the church," the deputy told Vincent sternly. "If and when she decides she wants you, she'll be along."

"Not if he was the last man in Colorado," Kylie snapped.

The deputy smothered a chuckle with a cough behind a fist. Kylie quelled the urge to poke him for making her think that he might arrest her. Instead, a relieved sigh gusted out of her.

It wasn't easy for Vincent to back down, and she well knew of the enmity between his branch of the family and old George's. As soon as she'd realized the identity of this big man, she'd half expected the situation to devolve to fisticuffs. To "cousin" Zach's credit, he'd managed to stop Vincent with wit rather than brawn.

Clearly thwarted, Vincent dithered for a bit before swinging around to stride angrily back toward the church, declaring, "This isn't over!"

He shot a vicious glare at her father as he passed. Her dad sighed and shoved a hand through his thinning hair before trudging forward.

"Kylie, honey," he said apologetically, "I'm so sorry. I knew that boy was no-account, but you had your heart set on him and—"

"Oh, Daddy." She stepped out from behind the deputy to go to her father. "It's not like that. I—I mean, I was willing to marry him. That is, I thought… It seemed like God's will at the time, with the business and all."

He caught her in his beefy arms and hugged her to him. "Kylie, I tried to tell you that my business with Samuel has nothing to do with you and Vincent."

"It's just that Vincent guaranteed Samuel would buy out your share of the ranch if we married."

"Even if that were true," her father argued, shaking his head, "it wouldn't be enough to pay off the loan, not with real estate prices falling. God will take care of us, honey. Believe it!"

"May not be my place to say so," the deputy spoke up, "but

if you're in business with my great-uncle Samuel, you've got enough trouble without bringing Vincent into your family."

"I'm sure you're right about that," her father agreed, putting out a hand. "Gene Jones of Jones Feed & Supply."

As he stepped forward to take that hand, the deputy glanced across the green to the feed store on the other side of the tracks north of Railroad Street.

"Used to be Wilmont's Feed & Supply back in the day."

"We bought him out six, seven years ago."

"I was long gone by then. Zach Clayton, Deputy Sheriff." He tipped his hat to the bride and smiled, displaying a single dimple.

Oh, my. Vincent was about to be dethroned as the best-looking Clayton around town. "Kylie Jones."

"Kylie Jeanne Jones, if I'm not mistaken."

She nodded, reaching up with both hands to pluck the combs from her hair and sweep off the veil. Her hair had been rolled up on both sides and pinned at the back of her head with a heart-shaped rhinestone clip, leaving the rest to hang down her back in spiral curls.

"Would you really have arrested me?"

"You and Vincent both," he answered honestly. "If pressed to it." Grinning, he added, "I think you'd have gotten off. Him too, probably. But the report would've gone into the papers just the same."

"And you knew Vincent wouldn't want that."

The lawman nodded and said, "You found A.J. Wesson."

"That's right."

"I'd like to talk to you about that."

"Now?" Kylie asked, holding out her satin skirts.

"You seem to have something more important to do," he conceded. "But soon. Next week for sure."

Dropping her skirts, she sighed. "That's fine." She looked

to her father, saying, "Right now, I guess one of us better get back to the church and tell everyone that the wedding is off."

Gene patted his daughter's shoulder. "I'll see to it, honey, while you talk to your mother and sister in private."

"Thank you, Dad." Leaning in, she kissed his cheek. "I'm sorry about all this."

"It's just as well, if you ask me. Better to find out he's unfaithful now than after you'd married him."

Kylie nodded, suddenly weary despite the great sense of relief that swept over her. To think that she had very nearly married Vincent Clayton! She felt as if she'd just awakened from a long, confusing dream.

Lifting her skirts, she began making her way back across the grass, but then she remembered that the new deputy wanted to talk to her about how she'd found A.J. that day. She paused and glanced his way. He was one big, handsome man, all right—but he was also a Clayton, and all the Claytons with whom she had dealt had turned out to be trouble. Nevertheless, this one wore a badge.

"Our place is out on Waxwing Road," she told him.

"I'll be around."

"Okay, then. Oh, and thank you."

He doffed his cap. "My pleasure, Miss Jones."

She turned to make her way back across the green. She didn't relish what was to come, but the unspeakable relief that she felt told her that she was doing the right thing. Recalling that she'd recently asked God to settle her doubts for her, she had to smile. Like her mama always said, be careful what you ask for.

Stepping up into the tiny mudroom of the frame house on Bluebird Lane where he had grown up, Zach set down his luggage and hung his cap on a peg. The house had been closed for several years before his sister Brooke had moved in a few weeks earlier. Her silver Toyota Corolla sat beside his Jeep out in the drive, so presumably he'd find her at home and not next door with her fiancé, Gabe. Zach walked into the kitchen, where he paused beside the long, low, narrow island that served as the breakfast table. Five round-backed chairs flanked it on three sides.

At one time, there had been six.

Zach tilted his head, listening. The whir of a hair-dryer came to him from the vicinity of the bathroom off the hallway to his left. Grinning, Zach sauntered in that direction, calling out, "Honey, I'm home!"

The dryer shut off, clattering in the sink. He jumped back as the bathroom door burst open. He'd learned that trick the hard way as a kid when the sudden opening of the door had caught him square in the face and raised a bump the size of a goose egg on his forehead. He no longer had the goose egg, but it had engendered a family nickname that his sisters still used even now.

"Lump! You came!" Wearing a bathrobe over shorts and a tank top, she threw her arms around his neck.

"Hey, Gigglebot." He returned the greeting by hugging her hard enough to lift her off her feet.

A swatch of her long blond hair clung damply to one side of her face, and she wore not a speck of cosmetics, but the happiness shining in her blue eyes made her utterly beautiful. Zach smiled.

Pulling back, she looked him over. "So you did it," she said. "You took the job as deputy sheriff. Never thought I'd see it."

Zach shrugged. "Timing was right."

Miami had become untenable for Zach, then suddenly Linden Diggers had retired as deputy sheriff, leaving the satellite office in Clayton vacant. Given that, the absurd stipulation in his grandfather's will, which required each heir to live a year in Clayton, and Vincent starting to stir up trouble again, Zach had decided to step into old Diggers' boots for a while, just as his late grandfather had proposed. That the old man had been keeping tabs on him galled Zach, but George Sr.'s taped message to his grandson had proved that he had been well aware of all that had happened in Miami, though Zach had not shared that information with anyone in the family. What good would that do? What mattered now was helping his cousins claim their inheritances, five hundred acres and a quarter million dollars each.

"You caught me all a mess," Brooke said, touching her hair self-consciously.

"I have never seen you looking better," Zach told her sincerely. "You look…happy."

She laughed, that tinkling giggle warming his heart all the way through. "I am."

Zach smiled. Before their baby sister Lucy had died, at only two-and-a-half years of age, Brooke had run around the house laughing and singing all the time. Afterward, he'd had to tickle her to hear anything approximating that little girl giggle, but it had never been the same. She'd blamed herself for Lucy slipping out of the house and going to the creek. All these years later, he was beyond grateful to hear that happy, joyous sound again. It meant that she had forgiven herself at last.

"He must be quite a guy, this Gabe Wesson."

"Oh, he is. I'm getting ready to go out to dinner with him and A.J. Why don't you come with us? He's anxious to meet you."

I bet he is, Zach thought. Zach had called Gabe for a little man-to-man talk after he'd accused Brooke of being negligent in the disappearance of his young son, who Kylie Jones had found in Vincent's backyard. Brooke had phoned Zach in tears. In full big-brother mode, Zach had rung up Gabe. Now

Brooke and Gabe were engaged, and Zach was prepared to let bygones be bygones, provided Gabe was all he seemed.

"Just let me shower and change out of these clothes. Diggers left the office a mess, and I've been working on it all day."

"Take Mama's room. I cleaned it out for you. That way Viv and I won't have to share when she gets here."

If she gets here, Zach thought, but he didn't bother saying as much. She would come or she wouldn't. Same with Mei and Lucas. Still, Brooke had wisely made provision. She and Vivienne had shared a room as girls, but as women they obviously needed a measure of privacy, provided, of course, that Vivienne eventually showed up. But that worry could be left for later.

"I'll be ready before you will," Zach taunted, grinning.

"True!" Brooke laughed, spinning back into the bathroom.

Zach smiled to himself. It felt surprisingly good to be home.

Chapter Two

He'd known good times here, but tough ones, too, Zach told himself as he carried his luggage to his room, especially when it came to Lucy and his late father. George Jr. and his twin brother Vern, Zach's uncle, had died in an auto accident when Zach was twenty, some five years after Lucy's drowning. Zach's mother, Marion, had followed only a few years ago. After her funeral, Zach had intended *never* to return here.

Now, at thirty, he was moving back into the old house. Temporarily. After the required year here, Zach had every intention of heading back to his real life, wherever that might be. He expected that his sister Vivienne and most of his cousins would do the same, especially Lucas, who couldn't wait to get out of Clayton in the first place and hadn't even returned for their grandfather's funeral.

That reminded Zach that he still hadn't heard from or about Lucas. He had an old friend with the Florida state police putting feelers out unofficially, but so far he'd learned nothing. Uneasiness prickled the skin on the nape of Zach's neck, and he sent up a quick prayer that whatever was going on with his younger cousin would be resolved soon and safely. He feared not only for Lucas but also for their cousin

Arabella, who lived in Grandpa George's house with her triplet daughters, Jessie, Julie and Jamie, and her ward, Jasmine Turner. Arabella had taken care of their grandfather for years and deserved to inherit the house, but that would only happen if George Sr.'s other grandchildren gave up a year of their lives to fulfill the terms of the old man's will. Zach could only pray, for her sake, that everyone could and would.

Unzipping his bags, he first stowed his personal carry gun in the drawer of the bedside table before quickly unpacking. As he worked, he wondered idly when he would see Kylie Jeanne Jones again. Maybe he'd go out to the Jones place after the Fourth. It seemed likely that she would lay low for a few days after canceling her wedding to one of the town's most prominent sons.

Zach couldn't understand why Kylie had ever agreed to marry Vincent in the first place. All that talk of a buy-out was just so much nonsense. Samuel never parted with a nickel of his own if he could get someone else to do so first. Besides, from what Brooke had told him and what he'd seen already, Vincent hadn't changed much. Even if Brooke's fears and suspicions should prove unfounded—and Zach was too good a cop to let his personal prejudices decide the matter for him—Vincent still seemed to be the sly bully that he'd always been.

After stowing his empty bags in the closet, Zach removed his service gun, holster and belt, tucking them into the top drawer of his mother's empty dresser. All the while, he considered Kylie Jones.

She was an attractive little thing, with that waist-length cloud of light-golden-brown curls, those moss-green eyes and perfect lips. He thought of the finely boned shoulders and long slender arms displayed by the strapless wedding gown, the neatly nipped in waist and the flare of the full skirt.

Attractive? Who was he kidding? She was beautiful,

breathtakingly so in her wedding gown. Much too beautiful for the likes of Vincent.

At least she'd come to her senses in time to save herself. For now. The question was whether she'd stick to her guns or let Vincent wear her down, as he would surely try to do. Vincent didn't like to lose, even if the "prize" was something he didn't really want. Zach hoped that Kylie would be smart enough to keep her distance from Vincent, which was probably good advice on his end, too.

The last thing Zach needed was trouble with Vincent and that side of the family, especially since Vincent's father Pauley had managed to get himself elected mayor. *Thankfully,* Zach thought, *I answer only to the county sheriff!*

After a quick shower, he changed into comfortable jeans and a simple navy blue T-shirt before performing a fast shave and sweeping his short, ash-brown hair straight back from his brow. He saw that the barber hadn't quite gotten all of the lighter tips on the top of his head, where the Florida sun had bleached his hair almost blond. That made the contrast between his hair and his darker brows all the more pronounced. No matter. Another trim would take care of it.

He wondered how soon his tan would fade. Probably not for a few months. He recalled that Kylie Jones had smooth, ivory skin, with just a smattering of freckles on her cheeks. Turning off that thought, he pulled on a pair of black cowboy boots. Then he took the compact 9 mm from the drawer in the bedside table and slipped it into the holster hidden in the small of his back, making sure that it was secure and easily accessible. By law, all peace officers were required to carry a handgun when off-duty. It seemed unnecessary around here, but Zach would have felt naked without the thing. And he had learned the hard way how helpless a cop could be without firepower.

Properly dressed, he went to the kitchen and helped

himself to a cold glass of water. Brooke came out of her room
a few minutes later dressed in patriotic style, the softly gathered skirt of her red-white-and-blue plaid sundress swirling
about her ankles.

"Come on. Gabe's waiting!"

Chuckling, Zach left the glass in the sink and walked his
sister next door to meet the man who had put that silly smile
on her face.

Though a wealthy businessman from Denver, Gabe turned
out to be unexpectedly down-to-earth. His home displayed a
certain tasteful affluence well above the norm around Clayton, but Gabe himself came off as an average guy. The look
in his eyes when he welcomed Brooke told Zach that Gabe
felt as much for Brooke as she did for him. Best of all, Gabe's
little boy flew into the room and literally threw himself at
Brooke's knees. She lifted him up onto her hip with such fond
ease that Zach found himself clearing away a sudden lump
in his throat.

He'd prayed to see Brooke as at ease with a child as she
appeared to be with this one. After Lucy's death, Brooke
had vowed never to have children of her own. Now here she
stood, rubbing noses with little A.J. and making goo-goo eyes
at him while Gabe looked on with fierce pride and obvious
love.

They moved into the living room to visit for a few minutes. Talk centered on the day's events, starting with Zach's
swearing in that morning and culminating with the breakup
of Vincent and Kylie. Though shocking, the news that the
wedding had not taken place pleased Brooke.

"We weren't invited, of course, being from George's side
of the family, but I couldn't help wondering if she knew what
she was getting into."

The two brothers—George Sr., Zach's grandfather, and
Samuel, Vincent's grandfather—had come to a parting of

the ways more than fifty years ago. Sadly, the two sides of the family considered themselves enemies.

"Kylie was very kind that day," Gabe said, stroking A.J.'s tiny head. The boy had gone missing while in Brooke's care and been found by Kylie a quarter mile away in Vincent's backyard.

Eventually the little party began forming up to leave. "So, where are we going for dinner?" Zach asked.

Brooke and Gabe looked at each other, then turned as one to him. "To the Cowboy Café. Where else?"

Zach chuckled. He had thought that they might drive over the mountain to one of the more touristy communities with their review-rated restaurants. Evidently, his little sister had well and truly settled back in Clayton. Leaving town hadn't even occurred to her.

Some minutes later—getting a child into and out of a vehicle proved to be more complicated than Zach had realized—Zach followed his sister, Gabe and A.J. into the little café in downtown Clayton.

The old place hadn't changed, despite the little American flags peppering the place. A couple hands from the ranches outside of town turned on their stools at the counter running down one side of the long, narrow room to see who had come through the door. Others sitting at the rustic tables crowded into the front of the room looked up to wave or nod as a raucous country and western tune blared from the jukebox near the door.

Gabe and Brooke chose a table in one corner near the antique cash register at the end of the counter, helping themselves to a battered booster seat along the way. While they settled A.J., Zach shook hands with an old schoolteacher who had recognized him. He'd barely put his backside to the chair when a slender dervish in skinny blue jeans and a red T-shirt plunked down glasses of water, including a plastic cup with a lid for the toddler. The long, golden-brown braid hanging down her back swung across her shoulder as she bent to bring her face close to A.J.'s.

"Hi, sweetie! How are you? Gerald's made up some mac and cheese that you ought to love." She tapped the tip of his nose with a bare, neatly trimmed fingernail and straightened. "Meatloaf to go along with it for the rest of you, if you're interested."

Feeling a jolt of combined recognition and surprise, Zach blinked at the waitress. She blinked back at him. At almost the same instant, they both blurted, "You!"

Obviously, Zach had underestimated Kylie Jeanne Jones. This morning she'd canceled her wedding, and this evening she served tables in the most public venue in town, sans the fake fingernails. No shrinking violet here. Just a very pretty one.

Zach couldn't help smiling.

Sitting at home and indulging in a pity party after her canceled wedding had not appealed to Kylie one bit. She knew from experience that, when disappointment derailed one's plans, keeping busy helped. That's what she'd done since leaving college just months shy of graduation to come back here and help out at home financially.

She'd thought marrying Vincent would ease her family's situation, but after spotting him making out with another woman in a parked car in the lot at the church where she had just arrived for their wedding, she hadn't been able to go through with it. She felt surprisingly relieved about canceling the ceremony, even though it meant that her family would continue to need her wages to keep from losing their business. All things considered, after the debacle at the church, picking up an extra shift at the café had seemed like the thing to do. However, she hadn't expected to bump into the one individual, besides her dad, who had actually witnessed the humiliating scene with Vincent today.

The deputy sheriff's good looks struck her again. The dark blue of his eyes almost matched his navy shirt, and his smile carved that single dimple in the lean plane of his cheek. Brows and lashes a shade darker than his light brown hair, which the sun had bleached gold at the tips; a strong, straight nose and wide mouth completed the picture.

"I understand you've met my brother," Brooke said wryly.

Kylie's head snapped around. "This one's your brother?"

Brooke inclined her head, eyes shining. "That's our Lumphead. Better known as Zach."

"Watch it, Gigglebot," he shot back.

She smiled, and Kylie realized that Brooke had the same dimple. Funny, she'd never noticed that before, and she'd known Brooke since high school. She'd known, too, somewhere in the back of her mind, that Brooke had an older brother, but he'd been long gone by the time Kylie had come to Clayton.

"Then I guess your brother's told you…" She waved a hand, unwilling to say more about canceling the wedding here in the diner. Everyone knew, of course, but they were curbing their curiosity out of sheer civility.

Brooke nodded. "To tell you the truth, I'm relieved."

"Why is that?" Kylie knew how deep the animosity ran on both sides of the family, but she couldn't imagine why Brooke would be concerned for her one way or another. It had been years since they'd been even casual friends, and Kylie had put herself in the enemy camp, so to speak, by becoming engaged to Vincent.

For answer, Brooke just glanced at her brother, who drawled, "Because no woman in her right mind would get involved with Vincent."

Kylie stiffened. "Oh, really?"

Today's events had left her emotions raw, and the criticism sounded particularly harsh coming from the man she'd been thinking of as her personal hero. Obviously, his intervention today had been all about sticking it to Vincent rather than rescuing her.

At the tone of her voice, Zach Clayton frowned. "I didn't mean—"

Kylie interrupted him, stung and embarrassed. "What can I get you folks? I highly recommend the special, but it's up to you."

Gabe flashed Zach a sympathetic look and said, "Meatloaf sounds great to me."

They all ordered the meatloaf. Gabe and Brooke chose iced tea with theirs. Zach preferred a cola.

Kylie tried not to glare at him. She didn't care what he had to drink or know why his comment bothered her so much. Yet, for some reason she especially resented hearing her rescuer describe her as "not in her right mind." At least he had the decency to look uncomfortable about it. Well, that made two of them.

"Suit yourself," she barked, hurrying away.

She regretted her tone immediately. Maybe coming to work had been a bad idea after all. Feeling weary, she suddenly wished that it had been anyone but Zach Clayton standing there in that uniform today. She'd have much preferred old Diggers to have witnessed her humiliation. Then again, Diggers might not have even intervened. Everyone knew that he and Pauley, Vincent's father and the town's part-time, unpaid mayor, were thick as thieves.

Besides, she had much bigger problems than a little embarrassment. No matter what her father said, Kylie knew that he'd been counting on Vincent's grandfather to buy out his share of the ranch in which they'd invested together. If only her dad hadn't followed Samuel's advice and put up Jones

Feed & Supply as collateral for the loan. If only he hadn't bought into the ranch with Samuel in the first place. If only Vincent could have been trustworthy. If only…

Sunday morning dawned bright and beautiful. The doves nesting in the bigtooth maple outside her open bedroom window cooed and gurgled in the cool morning air.

Kylie rolled onto her back, shoving away the covers on her bed, but she did not immediately rise. Zach Clayton's words from the night before had played through her head incessantly.

No woman in her right mind would get involved with Vincent.

Sadly, Zach Clayton had that right. Kylie could admit now that she hadn't been in her right mind when she'd agreed to marry Vincent.

Desperation had driven her to consider his proposal, but she had been wrong to accept. She didn't love him. She barely even liked him, but somehow she had convinced herself that she should marry him. Idiot that she was, she had believed that he cared for her and that he would, at the very least, be a faithful husband. Thankfully she had realized the truth before saying her vows.

Still, she had been a ninny to let it get that far. Oh, she'd told herself that she could change him, but in truth she'd gotten so carried away by her hopes for her family and her delight in planning the wedding that she'd almost forgotten that the price for those things would be a lifetime of marriage to Vincent.

She considered pulling the covers over her head and pretending that yesterday hadn't happened, but that would serve no purpose, and it might even make things worse. It would be best to show up at the church where she'd intended to be married with her head held high. Besides, her soul craved the healing balm of worship.

At least she need not fear running into Vincent there. Her ex had made it clear that he had little use for "organized religion." Actually, it would have been much more likely that he'd have appeared at the diner last night, but she hadn't considered that at the time. Thank goodness he'd apparently had something else to keep him busy last night. Or *someone.*

The door to the hallway opened, and her little sister bounced into the room. A cheerleader and distance runner, the energetic seventeen-year-old had a disposition as sunny as her long, yellow-gold hair. Kylie's own plain brown was crinkly curly, but Mariette's curls were as bouncy as Mariette herself. With eyes like jade instead of moss, Mariette outshone Kylie in every way, and Kylie couldn't have been more proud of her. Having graduated as valedictorian of her class, Mariette had landed a scholarship to a small college in New Mexico where she expected to run track, but Kylie knew the scholarship wouldn't cover everything. They'd all have to pull together to keep her sister in school.

"Oh, you're awake already," Mariette said. She dropped down onto the bed with one long, slender leg folded beneath her. "You look tired. Didn't you sleep well?"

Kylie sighed and shook her head. "I feel so stupid. I had convinced myself that Vincent was God's will for me, for all of us. I couldn't have been more wrong."

Mariette patted her hand. "It's okay, sis. Mom says maybe we can sell the dress. Technically, it was never *used,* you know. I mean, nobody got married in it."

Kylie laughed. "That's true. I wore it for maybe an hour." Finding the dress and planning the wedding had been the most enjoyable part of her engagement, and she knew any number of Internet sites where she could "remarket" the dress and decorations. Kylie had become something of an expert when it came to finding wedding bargains online.

Mariette popped up off the bed. "Mom's making a *huuuge* breakfast, so find an appetite. Okay?"

Kylie nodded, smiling. Usually they all fended for themselves. Lynette Jones worked side-by-side with her husband at the Feed & Supply, so no one expected her to run a short order kitchen at home. However, whenever anything threatened the family, whenever anyone needed support, she broke out the pots and pans. Grateful for a loving family, Kylie found, to her surprise, that she actually had an appetite this morning.

She went to the table twenty minutes later in her bathrobe, freshly showered, her wet hair streaming down her back.

"I'm glad not to have to face holidays with that slimy old man," she declared, meaning Samuel.

A smaller, leaner version of her own daughters, Lynette seemed trim and fit next to her husband's larger, rounder form. While his kinky blond hair thinned into nonexistence, her long, wavy locks had silvered to the point where the original golden brown had all but disappeared.

"Now, now, sugar pie," Gene said mildly, dipping his pancake into heated syrup. "You know what the lawyer said."

"Just because there's no proof," she retorted, "doesn't mean Samuel Clayton didn't cheat us. I don't care what he says— he had to know those assay reports were incorrect. He just wanted someone else to help him pay for his ranch." She exhaled sharply. "Now he's running cattle, and we're making payments on land we can't afford to use and no one wants to mine. At least we don't have to call him family."

Kylie had long known her mother's feelings toward Vincent's grandfather, but Samuel had not *forced* her father to take out that loan, after all. It did seem odd, though, that after seeking a partner for the venture, he'd come up with the cash to purchase cattle on his own. Meanwhile, Kylie's parents struggled with onerous loan payments. When it had become obvious that no mining company was interested in going after the smattering of silver on the place, Kylie had left college and come home to help. Together, she and her parents had caught up the payments and kept them current, but doing so left very little to spare. One bad month at Jones Feed & Supply and they'd be lost.

But, Kylie thought guiltily, if the business went to the bank, her father would have to move the family back to Denver to find work, and she would leave Clayton behind once and for all. Maybe she could finish school then and find a way to open that bridal shop in Denver that she'd always wanted.

"I thought Vincent was okay," her sister admitted, "but I'm glad you didn't marry him. He doesn't deserve you."

Kylie felt tears well up in her eyes. How selfish of her to think of her own desires and ambitions when her sister's remained at risk and her parents' business teetered on the brink of disaster!

"You wouldn't be at all prejudiced, of course," she managed, finishing up her breakfast.

"I certainly would," Mariette admitted with a cheeky grin.

Laughing despite herself, Kylie pushed back from the table and went to dress.

Almost an hour later, the entire family piled into the battered white, dualie pickup truck for the almost two-mile ride into town. Gene and Lynette had bought the small acreage and picturesque log house on Waxwing Road—along with the business in town—from Edison Wilmont and his wife, who had retired to Durango to be near their daughter. It was a beautiful place built only a decade or so ago after the original frame house had burned.

Kylie had been content here throughout high school, but

when she'd gone to Denver for college, she hadn't intended to return to Clayton except for visits. She'd planned a career in business, but only when she'd interned at one of the city's largest bridal shops had she found her calling. She loved putting together weddings and had quickly made up her mind that she wanted her own business as a wedding planner.

For the good of her family, she'd tried to put that dream aside when she'd agreed to marry Vincent, but now it came roaring back to life. Sadly, she didn't see that dream coming true anytime soon, but maybe things would be different once Mariette finished college. Until then, Kylie was well and truly trapped in Clayton, Colorado.

But it wouldn't always be that way, she promised herself, and she would never again compromise her dream. Doing so had been a grave mistake.

With that silent vow, she turned her thoughts elsewhere and immediately found herself wondering if Deputy Sheriff Zach Clayton would be in church today. Or did he, like the other Clayton men of her acquaintance, believe that he did not "need" to attend worship?

Knowing what he must think of her, she almost hoped that he would not be there. The day promised to be challenging enough. However, she hated to think that he was no different from Vincent. That would be sad, indeed. Sad and, in a way she didn't want to examine too closely, very disappointing.

Chapter Three

He had to hand it to her, Zach thought, watching Kylie Jones join the congregation in singing a patriotic hymn. Despite her shadowed eyes and less than animated expression, the girl seemed determined to stand her ground openly. Deep down, Zach admired her for that. Unfortunately, that hadn't kept him from making a ham-handed statement that had obviously offended her last night. And who could blame her?

He noted that her family seemed very supportive. That included the golden-haired teenager who hovered protectively at Kylie's side. Given the resemblance, Zach assumed the blonde to be Kylie's younger sister. Obviously, the girls took after their mother.

Like nearly everyone else in the building, Kylie had dressed in keeping with the Independence Day observance, but Zach couldn't help wondering if she'd chosen white deliberately. Of course, yesterday's ivory satin confection could not truly be compared with today's white denim skirt and sleeveless knit top emblazoned on one shoulder with a red star trailing a sparkly blue trail. Still, it reminded him of his first sight of her, a dream in satin flying across the corner of the greensward. He particularly remembered the way the hip-length veil had floated behind her as she'd run toward him.

He marveled at the length of her vibrant hair. Caught back with a wide, red, knit band at the crown of her head, the crinkly ends hung all the way to her narrow waist. His fingers itched to touch that hair, to test its texture and weight. It looked like a soft, misty, light-golden-brown cloud.

Realizing that he was not paying attention to the service, Zach shifted his gaze to the hymnal in his hand, following along as the others sang. Because his singing sounded like a bullfrog in full throat, he never joined in, but he'd found that *not* singing actually heightened his appreciation of the music and allowed him to concentrate more on the words. When he could keep himself from staring at a pretty girl displaying almost heroic bravery.

He managed to confine his gaze to a path between his Bible and the pulpit as the pastor delivered the sermon. Quite a sermon it turned out to be, too, referencing both the twelfth chapter of Mark, where Jesus was asked about paying taxes, and the Gospel of John, Chapter two, which described Jesus driving the money changers from the temple. The pastor managed to tie both together into a coherent argument for patriotic duty superseded only by righteous zeal.

Having met the man just twice, once a few years earlier at his mom's funeral and again recently at his grandfather's, Zach knew Reverend West only slightly. The pastor had some interesting ideas and seemed a vibrant presence in the little church, which had become, in many ways, the hub of the town. Brooke had told him that the reverend, rather than the mayor, had even spearheaded the community-wide picnic on the green. Otherwise, she'd said, the Independence Day tradition would have died. Some city head Pauley had turned out to be if the pastor of the church had been required to step in and plan a community event.

At the end of the service, Zach made it to the door well ahead of Kylie and her family simply because he'd been sitting closer to the back of the sanctuary. Reverend West, a tall, bulky man in his forties with the build of a football player, warm brown eyes and thick, caramel-colored hair, gave Zach's hand a hearty shake and welcomed him to town in his capacity as the deputy sheriff.

"It's good there was no lapse in assignment," he said. "Clayton's no worse than any other small town, I suppose, but I think many are comforted to know that we didn't have to wait months for a replacement deputy."

"Guess it's God's timing, as my mother would say," Zach replied with a smile.

"Yes, Marion would say that," the pastor, whose first name was John, agreed.

Zach stepped to one side, and they chatted a few moments more between other handshakes and greetings until Zach moved farther away.

"Glad to have seen you here today," the pastor told him, turning to give a frail, elderly woman his attention.

She looked rather like old Mrs. Rader, only even smaller and more wizened. She seemed distressed. The pastor bent low to listen to what she had to say. Zach hovered at a polite distance, his senses alerted to trouble, while Brooke and Gabe visited and laughed with friends at the bottom of the steps.

Zach first realized that Kylie had slipped past the traffic jam in the doorway when she appeared at his elbow and muttered what sounded like, "It's her granddaughter."

Copying Reverend West, Zach bent his head to her in an attempt to provide some privacy. "I beg your pardon?"

"Mrs. Rader."

"Ah. I thought that was her."

"She's concerned about her granddaughter. Seems Sherilyn didn't come home last night."

"I see." He glanced at the elderly woman. "Maybe I should introduce myself."

Kylie shrugged. "If you're going to search for Sherilyn, start at Vincent's."

"Vincent's?"

"She was in the car with him yesterday." Turning to gaze out over the parking lot, Kylie nodded. "Right over there."

"She's the one you caught him with," Zach surmised quietly.

"Yep." Kylie moved toward the steps, and he ambled up beside her.

"Miss Jones."

"Hm?" Kylie asked.

"About what I said last night... I didn't mean that as an insult. I spoke without thinking."

She glanced at him, nodded and dropped her chin. "I know."

"I didn't mean to imply that you aren't... Weren't..."

"In my right mind," she supplied helpfully, stepping down.

"It's just that I spent my entire childhood around Vincent," he said, keeping up with her, "and I've seen some things beneath his charming exterior that..." He broke off, realizing with some puzzlement that he had said more than he normally would have. Feeling oddly exposed, he pulled his sunshades from his coat pocket and slid them on.

She sent a look up at him from beneath the thick sweep of her lashes. "You were right," she said quietly. "I was foolish and desperate."

Uncertain what to say to that, he simply stared at her until she stepped down onto the ground and walked toward his sister's party. Zach followed, automatically reconnoitering the area, noting who got into which car and who stood and gabbed with whom. Brooke and Gabe now chatted with a thin redhead and a little girl, maybe nine or ten years of age, wearing pink eyeglasses. As Kylie approached, the woman and child turned to greet her. The woman looked older than he'd first assumed her to be and seemed conspicuously frail. The child resembled a blond, blue-eyed doll.

"Do you know the Perrys?" Kylie asked. Zach shook his head as Brooke made the introductions.

"This is Darlene and her daughter, Macy."

"Hello."

"My brother, Zach."

"Oh, you're the new deputy sheriff," Darlene said. "Nice to meet you."

"Likewise."

The girl shaded her eyes with a hand and looked up at him shyly. "You're tall."

"Mmm-hmm, and you're pretty."

She gave him a tiny smile and then ducked her head bashfully. Suddenly recognition hit him square in the chest. He looked at his sister then at Gabe and Kylie, but obviously none of them saw it. They wouldn't, of course. How could they know that Macy Perry, with that long blond hair, bright blue eyes and single dimple in her left cheek, looked exactly like Brooke at the same age? Or did his mind play tricks on him? Maybe being at home again had colored his perceptions, but his cop sense told him otherwise.

Talk turned to the Independence Day picnic. Kylie said something about having to serve food, but Zach listened with just half an ear while trying not to stare at Macy Perry. It wasn't unusual for two unrelated people to look alike, of course, but in a town filled with Claytons, such resemblance did not seem random. Who, he wondered, glancing around at the thinning crowd, was Macy Perry's father?

Shoving the flimsy, disposable aluminum pan back into Kylie's hands, Jerome shook his head. "That's perfectly good meat. Serve it."

"It's all fat!" Kylie protested.

Unlike Gerald, his happy-go-lucky, roly-poly brother, Jerome was tall, rail thin and as cheap as chewing gum. Both were excellent cooks. Neither, however, could make beef fat palatable.

Erin Fields, the owner of the Cowboy Café and their boss, breezed by, her long, copper-red ponytail flashing out behind her. Snatching the pan from Kylie's hands, she carried it away, saying, "You're just cooking the meat, Jerome, not paying for it. We'll make this pan an Independence Day treat for the local dogs." With that, she hurried toward the serving tables being set up on the green.

Jerome rolled his eyes disapprovingly and turned back to the enormous wheeled grill. Built into a trailer frame, it had been towed to the edge of the street in front of the diner for easy access. The huge chunks of beef, donated by one of the local ranchers, had been smoking on the grill since six o'clock the previous evening, making dogs howl all over town. Erin and her employees had volunteered to serve it.

Kylie moved to the steel worktable that had been moved out of the kitchen and set up beneath a bright blue canopy tent. Humming, Gerald busily sliced smoked meat with an enormous knife and mechanical precision, piling the slices into a series of disposable pans. Kylie covered one with tin foil and carried it across the street toward the serving tables. Ahead of her, Vincent sauntered by with Sherilyn Rader on his arm.

They'd been burning up the edge of the green nearest the diner all afternoon, strolling back and forth, over and over again. Apparently, Vincent found it necessary to flaunt his girlfriend in public to save face. At first, Kylie hadn't recognized Sherilyn because the silly thing had dyed her streaky chestnut hair an unnatural black. Despite studiously refusing to acknowledge the pair's existence, Kylie couldn't help noticing that Sherilyn wore next to nothing. Her outfit seemed to consist of flip-flops, a white sports bra and denim short shorts. She made Kylie feel positively overdressed in her usual work clothes: athletic shoes, jeans and a T-shirt, red in honor of the holiday. She'd wisely added a white visor, which meant that she could avoid looking at Vincent by just dipping her head slightly.

The next couple hours passed in a flurry of activity as Kylie and her coworkers laded the tables and served hundreds of pounds of mouth-watering, slow-cooked beef, which the diners carried back to their picnic spots and augmented with their side dishes of choice. Many of them actually carried the meat home with them and ate it there, several of them admitting that they'd be back to watch the fireworks being readied over at the football field. Zach came through near the end of the line, smiling behind his sunshades and carrying two large disposable platters.

He lifted the one on his right and said, "For me, Brooke, Gabe and A.J." Shoving forward the platter atop his left palm, he explained, "This one's for Arabella and her crew."

Arabella Michaels was another Clayton cousin. The divorced mother of triplets baked for the diner, and everyone greatly appreciated her offerings. Kylie started piling on the meat.

"Is Jasmine with Arabella?"

"Yep."

In addition to her own three kids, Arabella had taken in a teen abandoned by her drunk of a father. Jasmine Turner, who had recently become engaged to marry Cade Clayton, a first cousin to Vincent. Neither side of the family seemed thrilled by that relationship, but wherever Jasmine could be found, Cade would likely be, so Kylie kept piling on the meat until Zach chuckled and moved the first platter out of her reach.

"Enjoying yourself?" she asked idly, filling the second

platter while she eyed his dark green uniform shirt, which he wore today with blue jeans and boots.

"Sure. How about you?"

"Too busy. I'll enjoy myself after the meat's all gone."

"Pity," he said.

"Aw, I don't mind." She could've let him go then but found that she didn't really want to. Despite what he'd said on Saturday night, she liked this gorgeous man. Not only had he been in church on Sunday, he'd apologized for his remark and then he'd stood around worrying about poor old Mrs. Rader. Besides, something about his smile made her smile, so she asked, "Are you working, too?"

He dipped his chin in a nod. "I am."

"Wasn't sure. I mean, you're wearing the shirt but not the rest of the uniform, and you're not carrying your gun."

Leaning forward, he confessed, "Frankly, I'm not keen on the uniform. Too many years in plain clothes, I guess." He looked at her over the rim of his shades, his dark-blue eyes gleaming, and quietly added, "As for the gun, it's a law that a peace officer has to go armed in public at all times. Just because you don't see a firearm, darlin', doesn't mean I'm not packing one."

"Oh," Kylie squeaked, undone by his nearness, the deep, smoky timbre of his voice and that perfectly meaningless word "darlin'."

A microphone whined, and they both looked to the gazebo in the center of the green as Reverend West stepped up to speak. The crowd quickly hushed. Red, white and blue bunting ruffled in the breeze as he welcomed the crowd and led them in eloquent prayer before introducing the mayor. As soon as Pauley pulled a sheaf of folded paper from his pocket, everyone went back to what they'd been doing before the pastor had spoken.

Zach spoke out of the side of his mouth. "Guess we know who commands the respect around here."

Kylie said nothing, but she couldn't stop a smile from breaking across her face. Chuckling, he moved off then, and Kylie nodded at the blue-haired matron waiting behind him, her handbag dangling from one wrist, cardboard platter in hand. When the woman's narrowed gaze cut to a loudly laughing Vincent, Kylie realized that the woman had overheard every word of her conversation with Zach, most likely weighing every word for gossip potential.

As if to prove that assumption, the woman thrust forward her platter, remarking, "Those Clayton boys make fine-looking men, don't they?"

Kylie hummed a noncommittal reply and dished out the beef. Fine-looking men, indeed. She glanced surreptitiously from Zach to Vincent. Handsome, yes, but at least one of them had proved himself to be a jerk. Her gaze moved back to Zach, following him across the green. It remained to be seen whether the other was as fine as he looked.

By the time Kylie found herself free to enjoy the day, it had all but ended. Just the barest lip of the sun clung to the horizon as she strolled across the grass toward her parents, who had placed their chairs on the church lawn, her father having been charged with opening the church to provide access to the restrooms in the tiny vestibule. A tall form fell into step beside her. Smiling, she glanced up at Zach Clayton, noticing that his jaws had taken on the faint shadow of a day's growth of beard. The slight stubble gave him a rakishly handsome appearance.

"Where you headed?" he murmured.

"Going to sit with my parents a while."

"That's good. I won't worry about you then."

Kylie stopped dead in her tracks. "Worry about me?"

He winced. "I, um…well, you've seen how Vincent's been acting."

"No, not really," she said. In point of fact, she'd done her dead level best *not* to notice what Vincent had been up to, but she felt a glow in the center of her chest at the knowledge that Zach worried about her. With all these people here, three or four hundred at least, tall, good-looking Zach Clayton had been keeping an eye on *her*.

Zach cleared his throat, but the eruption of a loud argument forestalled whatever he'd been about to say.

"I want to go now!" pleaded a brunette in red capris and a red-and-white-striped tank top.

"You will sit down and shut up until I'm ready!" a man bawled right in her face.

"Who is that?" Zach asked, turning in their direction.

"I want to go now!" the woman insisted plaintively.

Kylie wracked her brain. "Uh, Janey…Janey…" She shook her head, unable to find a last name.

"I said be quiet!" the man shouted, launching into a diatribe about whiny, self-centered women.

"That's Rob Crenshaw. He's about my age and a friend of Vincent's."

Nodding, Zach strode forward. Without thinking, Kylie followed, drawn by Janey's sobs. Zach didn't pause, just walked right up and threw his left arm around Rob's shoulders in what looked like a companionable gesture.

"Rob," he said calmly. "Rob Crenshaw."

That surprised the younger man enough to shut him up and have him turning a stupefied gaze on Zach.

"Do I know you?"

"Deputy Sheriff Zach Clayton. How do you do?" Zach said, offering his right hand for a shake. Rob automatically took that hand and then seemed to have some difficulty letting go again. Zach turned him and walked him several steps away from the woman. While the two of them spoke quietly—actually, Zach did most of the talking—Kylie went to Janey.

"You okay?" she asked, patting the other woman on the back.

Heavily freckled and wholesome-looking, with pale hazel eyes and sleek, chin-length, dark-brown hair tucked behind her ears, Janey sniffed and nodded, confessing in a small voice, "He gets like this every time he drinks."

"I thought alcohol wasn't allowed on the green."

"It's not. He showed up with a snootful."

Just then, Rob turned and lurched toward Janey. "We're going," he announced tersely, seizing her by the upper arm.

Kylie glanced at Zach, who stood with his hands at his hips, watching. "Do you want to go with him?" Kylie asked quickly.

For an instant, Janey hesitated, but then she nodded and let Rob pull her away. Zach watched to make sure Janey was driving. Then he removed his sunshades, folded them, stowed them in his shirt pocket and strolled toward Kylie. She turned as he drew near, and he once more fell into step beside her. They a put a few yards between them and the small crowd that had gathered to gawk.

"You handled that quite easily."

Zach shrugged. "A bully never expects anyone to stand up to him. He's surprised when people don't cower or slink away. If you know what you're doing, that can give you an upper hand."

"I guess the badge doesn't hurt, either."

"Not a bit," he admitted with a grin.

He walked her toward her parents. Reverend West stood waiting for them at the edge of the church lawn. Somehow, John West always managed to look as cool as a cucumber, and today proved no exception. His chinos held crisp creases, and the white of his Old Glory T-shirt fairly glowed in the fading light. He stepped forward at once, offering his hand to Zach and greeting Kylie with a nod.

"You two obviously work well together."

Zach seemed as eager as Kylie to quell talk that involved the terms "you two" and "together." They both began speaking.

"Oh, I was just talking to Janey."

"A little private conversation between me and Crenshaw."

"I wasn't involved in anything."

"It's my job. The badge does most of the work."

Reverend West laughed and stepped forward to drop one hand atop Zach's shoulder and the other atop Kylie's. "I have a couple of spots open on the helpline ministry team with our Church Care Committee."

Zach flashed a pained look at Kylie.

"Oh, I'm, uh, on call twenty-four hours a day."

"And I work shifts," Kylie put in quickly.

"One evening a week," West said, not in the least deterred. "I believe it will fulfill the voluntary community service requirement of the county sheriff's new community involvement initiative."

Zach twisted one corner of his lips into a wry grin. "So it will."

The reverend looked to Kylie, saying, "I'll speak to Erin. Make sure she doesn't schedule you to work during your assigned hours."

Kylie swallowed a sigh and nodded.

"I'll tell Martha to expect you for training this Wednesday after prayer meeting then." With that, West slid his hands into his pants pockets and strolled off in another direction, whistling complacently.

Backing up a step, Zach sent Kylie a loaded look and said, "Remind me to watch my step around him from now on."

"You and me both."

"He's slicker than suntan oil. Glad he's on the good side."

"There is that," she agreed with less enthusiasm than she probably should have displayed.

"Well, I'm working," Zach said after a moment, shooting a glance at her parents. "Best get back out there." He walked away with a nod and a wave.

Kylie let out her sigh in one long, tired breath and turned to face her parents, who had watched the whole thing from the comfort of their lawn chairs, bottles of cold iced tea in their hands. Seeing the look of consternation on her face, they both burst out laughing. After a moment, Kylie joined them. For more than a year she'd avoided Reverend West's enlistment campaigns, and now, in the blink of an eye, she'd been caught. Her gaze drifted across the green until it settled on Zach Clayton's broad shoulders. At least she had company in the trap.

Kylie sat down on the grass next to her parents. Over the next hour or so, they watched a steady stream of mostly women trek to and from the church. Finally, her mother rose from her chair. "Keep Dad company while I check the supplies in the bathrooms, will you? We don't want to be poor hosts, and things need to be stocked for Sunday."

Kylie pushed up to her feet and waved her mother back down. "No, I'll take care of it."

"You sure?" Lynette asked even as she sat again.

Nodding, Kylie started toward the church. She knew how hard both of her parents worked. She could do this one small thing for her mom.

"The extra supplies are in the closet behind the sanctuary," her father called. Kylie flapped a hand in acknowledgment and moved away. "It's open," he went on, "but you'll have to go into the building from the front."

She climbed the front steps and went into the building.

Crossing the small foyer, she passed through a door on the left. A quick check showed that the paper products were, indeed, running low. Kylie went out again and pushed through the double doors that closed off the darkened sanctuary. She could barely see, but she didn't turn on the overhead lights. Instead, she went around the edge of the large, pew-lined room and out again through a door behind the piano. She did turn on a light in the back room and propped the door open with a cloth-covered brick, placed there for that purpose, while she went to the far corner of the cluttered space.

Her father had often complained of the lack of a light inside the closet, but it hadn't been wired for electricity. Kylie unbolted the rarely opened back door and pushed it wide to let in as much light as possible before going into the closet to gather supplies. She carried them back to the vestibule and stocked the restroom, then returned to lock up and turn off lights. Just as she passed through the door behind the piano and into the storage area again, a hand clamped down on her wrist.

She knew at once who held her. Fear rose in her throat, and she instantly reached out to God with mind and soul.

Chapter Four

Gasping, Kylie wrenched away.

"Now, now," Vincent crooned, crowding her into a stack of padded chairs. "I just want to talk. After all, we were supposed to be on our honeymoon right now."

"I have nothing to say to you."

"Kylie, baby, listen. I made a mistake, but it's not Sherilyn I want." He dipped his head as if to kiss her.

"I made a mistake, too, Vincent," she ground out, placing both hands against his chest and shoving. It was like trying to move a brick wall. "I made the mistake of thinking I could be happy with you. Now please let me go!"

"I've been letting you go for months," Vincent grunted, yanking down her hands. "Maybe that's the problem."

"Let me go!"

"Don't push me, Kylie. I don't want to do something we'll both regret."

"Very wise," said another voice.

Kylie sagged with relief.

Vincent spun to face his cousin. "This is none of your business, Zach!"

"You want to be alone with him, Kylie?"

"No."

"Then it's my business," he said.

Vincent turned a fulminous glare over one shoulder. "You're going to regret that."

"Leave her alone, Vincent."

Suddenly, Vincent launched himself at Zach. The next instant he reeled across the room, bumping into a table crowded with seasonal artificial flower arrangements. Zach followed, pushing aside a flimsy lectern with one foot. Vincent came up swinging, but Zach caught his fist in one hand and stepped close.

"I'm armed, Vincent, and entitled to defend myself. Think about that."

Jerking away, Vincent stumbled backward. He fell against the corner of the closet and careened right out the back door, somehow managing to get down the steep stairs on his feet. Kylie moved forward without even realizing it until she stood crammed in the doorway shoulder-to-shoulder with Zach. Weaving and huffing, Vincent lifted a hand, pointing at them. Just then, Sherilyn came around the corner of the building.

"Vincent? What's happening?" She hurried over and tried to steady him. "You okay?"

Vincent shoved her away. Sherilyn reeled but didn't fall. Sparing not so much as a glance for her, he jabbed his finger at the doorway. "You two have embarrassed me for the last time!"

"You're embarrassing yourself, Vincent," Kylie said quietly.

He glared at her, but what she'd said seemed to sink in finally. Whirling around, he stalked off. Sherilyn ran after him. He could be heard growling, "Get away from me!" as Zach pulled the door closed.

Kylie shoved the bolt home and turned to put her back to the door, sighing. "Thank God you came when you did. Again."

"I saw him follow you inside," Zach explained. "By the time I could get over here…" He shook his head. "It was all I could do not to run, but I didn't want to attract attention. I won't hesitate next time."

Glad for that, Kylie nodded. Reaching out, he pushed the closet door closed. Kylie opened it again and twisted the lock in the center of the knob before closing it once more.

"What now?" Zach asked.

She pretended not to understand the question. "Now, we watch some fireworks."

"Okay," Zach said on a sigh. "Pressing charges against Vincent would do no good and probably make matters worse. Besides, no real harm occurred. I'll let it go. This time."

"I think that's best," she said, moving swiftly toward the sanctuary.

When she heard the clumps of Zach's boots on the floor behind her, she switched off the light and stepped out into the larger room. The darkness had deepened just in those few minutes since she'd crossed the space earlier. She groped her way past the piano then found herself slightly disoriented. A touch on her arm startled her, then his hand slid down and found hers. He tugged her forward. She followed gratefully, breaking the contact only when they reached the foyer.

Kylie waved her hand at the woman seated on the church lawn. "This is my mom, Lynette."

Zach dipped his head. "Ma'am."

"You must be Zach Clayton."

"Yes, ma'am. Nice to meet you."

"What was going on?" Gene asked, peering toward the deepening shadows at the rear of the building. "I thought I saw Vincent coming from back there."

"You'd have to ask him," Kylie said with a shrug, linking her arm through Zach's.

He managed not to start at the contact, the way she had when he'd taken her hand back there in the sanctuary. It had been an automatic gesture on his part, a way of saying that he was with her there in the dark. This…he didn't know what this was.

"Well, everybody's heading over to the football field," Gene noted, hauling himself out of his chair.

"My Jeep's parked over there," Zach said. "Guess I better follow the crowd."

"You kids go on and enjoy the fireworks," Mrs. Jones told them. "We'll lock up this place and watch from here."

To Zach's surprise, Kylie chirped a cheery "Thanks, Mom," and turned him toward the green. Zach plastered a smile on his face and gave her parents a parting wave.

"Come over to the Feed & Supply when you're done," Gene called as they walked away.

They had put all of ten feet between them and her parents before Kylie loosened her hold and softly said, "Thanks for not telling them about Vincent cornering me. My dad worries."

"He should," Zach said. "How did you get mixed up with Vincent, anyway?"

She sighed. "He started asking me out when I was in high school, but Dad thought he was too old for me back then."

Because he and Vincent were about the same age, Zach lifted his eyebrows at that. "How old are you?"

"Twenty-two."

That made her eight years younger than him. "Yeah, I can see why your daddy would think that. Then."

She nodded. "Well, as soon as I got back to town about a year ago, Vincent started asking me out again." She shrugged. "I didn't see why not. One thing led to another and eventually he asked me to marry him."

Zach nodded. Sounded perfectly reasonable, so why did

it chafe him? Clearing his throat, he asked, "What brought you back here?"

She sighed, reached behind her with her free hand and tugged her braid around to drape over one shoulder. "My father borrowed money to go into partnership with Vincent's grandpa, Samuel. The price of silver had bumped up, and Samuel had a lead on a ranch east of town with a rich assay report but not enough money to buy it outright." Zach could feel what was coming next, but he kept quiet and listened. "Turned out the assay reports were done ten years ago by a firm that's gone out of business. Dad didn't know until he started contacting mining companies, trying to interest them."

"They did their own assay reports, I assume."

She nodded. "And declined further involvement. Meanwhile, Samuel bought cattle and started running them on the land. Dad couldn't afford to do the same, so he's stuck making payments on the loan while Samuel plays rancher. For a while, it looked like Mom and Dad would lose everything because Dad had to put up the Feed & Supply as collateral on the loan. I dropped out of college and came home to help out."

Zach shook his head, drawing the only possible conclusion. "So when Vincent promised that Samuel would buy out your father's share of the ranch if you married him, you agreed."

"Something like that," she admitted softly. "Pretty stupid, huh?"

"Maybe." They'd walked all the way across the green. Zach drew to a halt at the corner of Hawk Street and Morning Dove Road, looking down at her. "It's also loyal, trusting and selfless."

She scoffed. "Hardly that. It looked like an easy way out, if you want to know the truth. I convinced myself that Vincent was the answer to my prayers. Like I said, stupid." She grimaced, adding, "It might have worked, if I'd really connected with Vincent, but I realize now that I was using him. I didn't even try to feel the way I should have."

"Whoa!" Zach gaped at her. "You're going to stand there and blame yourself? You caught him with another woman." He glanced around and lowered his voice, adding, "On your wedding day, for pity's sake."

Kylie lifted a hand to the top of her head. "I know. I guess it took that to wake me up, though." She shook her head, adding, "I don't even understand it myself, really. I never wanted to come back to Clayton. I was happy in Denver, and I've always intended to get back there, but with Mom and Dad's financial mess…" She shrugged.

"You wanted to help your family that much?" Zach asked, feeling humbled. Sure, he'd come back to Clayton to help out family, but he stood to gain, too. He couldn't positively say that he'd have come back if something hadn't been in it for him. That brought a twinge of shame.

Kylie lifted a hand. "Look, my little sister is heading to college in a couple months. She has a scholarship. Otherwise, it wouldn't be possible. But even with that, it's going to be a challenge."

"You gave up college so she could go."

"I just have a single semester to complete. I can do that anytime, online even."

"But you won't until she graduates."

Kylie didn't reply to that. Zach stood transfixed for a moment, caught by the purity of her beauty and the depth of her soul. He didn't even realize that he'd dipped his head and leaned toward her until a spray of gravel caught his attention. Jerking straight, he glanced around. Others also walked toward the football field, but some who had parked around the square tried to drive the block or so to the school grounds, resulting in what passed for a traffic jam in Clayton. No one seemed to pay them any attention. Besides, he had not almost kissed her just now. Really.

"I'm parked on Barn Owl between School Road and Goose Lane," he said, taking her by the arm and walking her along the edge of the green past the grocery. "We can watch the fireworks from the back of my Jeep."

"Oh, I didn't mean to rope you into keeping me company."

"I thought *you* were keeping *me* company." He gazed down at her. "Come on. Unless you prefer to sit in the stands."

She made a face. "I'm not big on imitating sardines."

Zach laughed. Because the stands on either side of the football field might accommodate a hundred people each, she could be right about the crowded conditions. Many would doubtlessly sit outside the chain-link fence around the field in their lawn chairs, but most would want the seats in the stands. Like her, Zach appreciated a bit of breathing room. They weren't the only ones. Vehicles of every description lined the street.

He nosed in on the north side. Swinging open the tailgate on the Wrangler, he sat on the bumper and stretched out his legs before him. He crossed his ankles and leaned back on his elbows. Kylie perched on the lip above the bumper and drew up her feet, folding her arms atop her knees. She asked why he'd moved back to Clayton, and he told her about his grandfather's unconventional will.

"So the other four have to come back, too, or no one inherits?"

"Three," he corrected. "Arabella has lived here all along, and Brooke and I are already in town. That leaves our sister, Vivienne, and our cousins, Lucas and Mei."

"What happens if they don't all show up?"

"The inheritance goes to Samuel."

"Oh, wow."

"Mmm-hmm."

Suddenly a hissing sound filled the air. The next instant, the sky exploded in a shower of red, white and blue stars.

After the *oohs* and *ahhs,* Kylie said, "Old George gave the city its fireworks every year, did you know that?" Zach shook his head. Obviously, he didn't know as much about his grandfather as he'd once believed. "I can't imagine Samuel doing that," Kylie muttered. "This could be the last time we'll get to do this."

"Could be," Zach agreed. He hoped not, though. As much as he'd resisted the idea of coming back to Clayton, he found something comforting about being in the midst of the community this way. It provided a feeling of continuity that he hadn't even realized he'd been missing.

Almost an hour passed with one breathtaking shower of colored light after another exploding against the night sky. The finale itself lasted a good five minutes. The instant the last firework faded, Zach got to his feet and helped Kylie do the same.

"Climb into the front seat. I'll take you over to the Feed & Supply, then come back here to help direct traffic."

"You sure?"

For an answer, he hurried around and opened the passenger door for her. She climbed in. After trotting around the front end of the Jeep, he got behind the steering wheel. Less than two minutes later, the Jeep bumped over the railroad track and into the yard at the Feed & Supply. Gene and Lynette Jones stood next to a dirty, white, somewhat battered, double-cab dualie. They waved as the Jeep came to a halt.

"Thanks again," Kylie said, opening her door.

Zach surprised himself as much as her when he reached across and clapped a hand onto her forearm. She sank back into her seat, her soft green eyes wide. Suddenly very aware of her parents watching them, Zach mentally gulped. His ears burned, and it felt as if he'd swallowed a hot coal.

"I just…well, I wanted to say that I'm glad you didn't go through with it. Marrying Vincent, I mean."

That moment back there on the corner came to mind, and he suddenly remembered calling her "darlin'" earlier in the day. She hadn't seemed to notice at the time, but if he didn't get a handle on his reaction to her, she would think he was hitting on her. Which he was. He couldn't seem to help himself!

She smiled and told him softly, "Me, too." An instant later, she closed the door. "You never did ask me about A.J.'s disappearance," she reminded him.

He felt like smacking himself between the eyes. Jamming the transmission into gear, he said gruffly, "I will."

First, though, he'd have to find his brain, not to mention a sizable dose of resolve. Common sense wouldn't go amiss either, he told himself as he drove away. Developing feelings for Vincent's runaway bride couldn't bring anything but trouble. He'd best keep his mind on his job and *off* Kylie Jeanne Jones.

The continued effort to decode his predecessor's filing system consumed the following morning for Zach, that and dealing with his father's cousin Pauley, who certainly had an inflated opinion of his importance as mayor. Time had not treated Pauley well. A small man, he appeared to be considerably older than the late fifties that he was. He swaggered into the deputy sheriff's office first thing and complained about the arrangement of the furnishings, calling it "unfriendly." He said this while leaning on the counter that Zach had placed at a right angle to the wall, thereby creating a small buffer zone between the door and the office proper. The file cabinets now lined the long wall in a neat row, and the desk sat at such an angle that Zach could see the computer screen, the door and the street beyond the window.

Zach chuckled, waved a hand at his father's cousin and said, "Take it up with the county," before going back to his stack of files.

Pauley stood around muttering for a few minutes then left, only to return an hour or so later to report that a cow of Wayne Bonner's had gone missing. Zach remembered Bonner as a grumpy rancher with a fascination for historical detail.

"Tell him to file a report."

"He's already filed a report," Pauley retorted pugnaciously. "With me."

"Then you take care of it."

Pauley went out sputtering that he was going to complain to the county sheriff that Zach wouldn't do his job. The sheriff called twenty minutes later to ask Zach to serve an old warrant having to do with a noise nuisance citation. On one Wayne Bonner. Zach happily complied. Maybe Pauley would think twice before making work for Zach again.

A grizzled old cowboy who lived a mile or so out of town, Bonner displayed an antique arsenal in his living room. When he saw the warrant, he spat tobacco into an empty green bean can, cursed Pauley Clayton and reported that the cow could be found climbing the mountain on an old elk migration trail.

"She'll come home when she gets tuckered. She always does."

"I see." So, Pauley had cooked up the whole thing, just as Zach had suspected. Next time he should pick a co-conspirator who didn't have a warrant out. "What exactly was the offense?" Zach asked, curious.

"Oh, it wasn't nothing," Wayne grumbled. "Just a demonstration of cannon fire. Wasn't even shooting balls. Not gonna risk a ball forged in 1860, I can tell you. If I'd been sober, nobody would've blinked an eye."

No wonder Diggers hadn't enforced the warrant. Zach, too, felt inclined to cut the old guy a break. Maybe then Pauley would back off. He called the county sheriff and arranged for Bonner to turn himself in the following Wednesday and pay a fine. The old boy looked like he'd swallowed his chaw of tobacco, but he nodded.

Zach drove back to town grinning, parked next to the county vehicle and walked across the green to take a late lunch at the Cowboy Café. He saw Kylie the instant he stepped through the door.

She laid plates in front of a pair of teenage boys at the counter, showing them a thousand-watt smile. Zach decided on the spot that the time had come to get Kylie's story about finding A.J. He walked to the very last stool against the wall and sat.

Kylie brought her smile to his corner. "Need some lunch? We have buffalo burgers and—"

"That'll do," Zach said, tucking away his sunshades.

She spun away, calling out, "Give me one with horns." Turning back to Zach, she pulled a cola from the cooler and set it down in front of him with a glass of ice. "Anything else?"

"Got a minute?"

She glanced around. "We're kind of busy."

A copper-haired young woman with a long ponytail moved from behind the cash register and toward them. Zach put two and two together and came up with a name.

"Erin, isn't it?" Erin Fields was the daughter of the original owners of the diner, but she'd been a kid of eleven or twelve when Zach had last seen her. She put her hand out, and he gripped it with his.

"And you're Zach Clayton. Glad to see you again."

"Thanks. I was wondering if I could have a word with Miss Jones."

Erin glanced around. "Sure. The worst of the lunch rush is past." She patted Kylie's arm, adding, "I'll cover you for a bit."

"Won't be long," Kylie promised.

"Take your time," Erin said lightly, turning away.

Kylie slipped out from behind the counter and came around to hitch up onto the stool beside Zach. He twisted the top off the soda bottle and began slowly pouring the soft drink over the ice in the glass.

"So what's up?" she asked.

He took his time, setting down the bottle and lifting the glass to sip the dark, bubbly liquid. "How are you? Still blaming yourself for the breakup when it was all on him?" Zach winced inwardly. When would he learn to keep his mouth shut?

"You would think that," she said with a slight smile.

Zach's gaze sharpened, his heart thumping. "What do you mean?"

"I know all about the bad blood between your side of the family and his."

Relaxing a little, Zach murmured, "I doubt that. At most, you know Vincent's take on the matter."

"He says your grandfather stole his grandfather's sweetheart."

Zach nodded. "My Grandma. Though Grandpa George didn't force her to choose him, you know, and it was more than fifty years ago, for pity's sake."

"Vincent also says George Sr. stole a bunch of money from his side of the family."

Zach sipped at his drink. "Grandpa was an attorney. He was the logical choice for my great-grandfather to pass the reins to, though I couldn't say how much money was involved. Don't you think, though, that if Samuel could prove money was stolen from him, he'd have already done so?"

She seemed to consider this. "I'm not sure Samuel would willingly invite the scrutiny of the law."

"Picked up on that, did you?"

She shrugged and changed the subject. "I don't think that's what you wanted to talk to me about."

"You're right. I want to know about the day that you found A.J. How did it happen?"

Her soft green eyes met his. "I was getting a drink of water in Vincent's kitchen and I heard something outside. I thought it might be a stray puppy or cat, so I went out back to check and found A.J. sitting in the dirt next to a bush at the corner of the house. He wasn't scared or crying, but he was pulling leaves off the bush. I called out to stop him from putting one into his mouth, and he was obviously glad to see me. I took him inside and called Sheriff Diggers. Then I cleaned him up and got him a drink."

"Was Vincent there?"

"Yes. We were going to watch a movie on DVD."

"Who arrived first, you or him?"

"He did. It's his house. I assume he was there all along."

Zach said nothing to that. "How did he act when you found A.J.?"

"I don't know. Sort of...amused."

"Uh-huh. How do you think A.J. got there?"

She bit her lip. "I assumed he had walked. When I think of the creek being right there..." She shuddered.

Zach mentally echoed that. "You really think a toddler walked a quarter mile alone, through the hedges and down along the creek?"

Kylie grimaced. "Doesn't seem likely, does it? But why would Vincent take the boy?"

Zach studied his glass. "Kylie, do you know what happened to my baby sister Lucy?"

"I heard something about a drowning and Brooke not watching her."

Zach nodded. "Lucy was just about A.J.'s age. Brooke was five years old. She and Lucy were watching cartoons in the living room when Mom went to take care of the laundry. She told Brooke to watch Lucy, but Brooke was caught up in her program. She didn't realize that Lucy had slipped out of the house and gone down to the creek until Mom came back. By the time Mom and Brooke found her, it was too late."

"Oh, Zach, I'm so sorry. I didn't realize."

"Brooke has always blamed herself."

"But she was only five!"

Zach nodded. "Until Brooke met Gabe and A.J., she was convinced that she shouldn't be a mother because of what happened."

Kylie clapped a hand to her forehead. "Brooke accused Vincent of taking A.J., but I didn't want to believe that Vincent could be so cruel. He called her irresponsible and said she ought not to be allowed around any child, but I thought that was bluster because she'd accused him of taking A.J. He must've known what that would do to Brooke."

"He knew exactly what that would do to Brooke," Zach concurred softly.

"But *why* would he do it?"

"To torment her. That's what he does. But also because of the will."

"You mean that he hopes to run her off before she can fulfill the stipulation of your grandfather's will."

"So the money will go to Samuel," Zach concurred. "At least that's the way I see it. If *any* of George's grandchildren fail to return to Clayton and stay for at least a year, then Samuel gets it all."

"Samuel won't let that money go easily," Kylie warned.

Taking a drink of his beverage, Zach nodded. After a moment, she asked, "What happens now?"

Swallowing a bitter lump, Zach shook his head. "Nothing happens now. There's no proof that Vincent had anything to do with A.J.'s disappearance."

Just then, Erin shoved a plate containing a burger and fries in front of Zach. She plunked down a bottle of ketchup and a knife and fork. "Can I get you anything else?"

"Nope. Looks great."

"Enjoy." She moved away again.

Kylie slid off the stool, saying, "Look, I don't want to get caught up in a Clayton family feud, but I thank God that the incident with A.J. didn't end in tragedy."

Thank God, indeed, Zach thought. More than one tragedy had been avoided around here lately, for that's what the marriage of Kylie Jones and his cousin Vincent would have been. Pure tragedy. Zach suffered no illusions, however. Like Samuel, Vincent did not easily let go of what he wanted, and his little stunt at the picnic proved that.

"I'd better get back to work," she said, edging away.

"Thanks for your time."

"Guess I'll see you tomorrow night."

"Oh, that's right," Zach returned lightly, as if he'd forgotten that they were expected at the church. In truth, he'd thought of little else, as foolish as that was.

Zach understood perfectly Kylie's reluctance to get between him and Vincent because he didn't particularly want to be between her and Vincent, either. But somebody had to keep a protective eye on Miss Kylie Jeanne Jones.

And if not the local deputy sheriff, he asked himself picking up his burger, then who?

Chapter Five

"It's mostly folks needing help to pay the electric bill or someone to check on an elderly parent," said plump Martha Ferber, her silver helmet of hair bobbing like a float on a fishing line. "Sometimes couples need counseling or their kids do."

Zach glanced over the list of agencies taped to the top of the table. "So, when someone calls the help line, we refer them to one of these groups."

Nodding, Mrs. Ferber went on. "Sometimes, they just want to talk, and sometimes they need to escape abuse. In that case, the most important thing is to stay calm. These folks call in a moment of crisis. To help them, we have to be sympathetic without being panicky. The cool head prevails." She punctuated that last statement with such a firm nod that her glasses slid perilously close to the end of her broad nose. Pushing them up again with a manicured fingertip, she went on in the brisk tone she had used as a teacher. "To be prepared, you'll want to study the script of possibilities in your information packet."

Zach set his teeth in his upper lip to keep from smiling. Here he sat, the big-city cop who had seen just about everything in his time, taking instruction on how to speak to an

abused caller from a retired schoolteacher about as wide as
she was tall, which wasn't saying much because Mrs. Ferber
barely reached his chest. Sitting next to him in a spindly
folding chair placed before a table laden with telephones and
computers, Kylie touched an elbow to his ribs and cleared her
throat. When he looked down, her clear green eyes sparkled
with mirth, but she deliberately frowned, making the point
that the subject deserved sincere attention. Shaking his head,
he looked away to keep from laughing.

"Am I going too fast for you, Zach?"

He cleared his throat. "No, ma'am. You're doing just fine."

Casting him a knowing, dismissive glance that made him
feel sixteen again, Martha Ferber went on detailing their
duties, which could not be called demanding by any means.
If an injury had occurred, an ambulance had to be called, but
because of confidentiality requirements, a client could only
be encouraged to notify the police. Zach privately thought it
unfortunate that the law did not require help lines to report
abusive situations to the police, but the victims of such abuse
rarely came forward and often would not seek even oblique
assistance if not guaranteed discretion.

The help line operated out of an office that opened onto
one end of the Fellowship Hall in "the Annex," a simple
structure erected at right angles to the west side of the sanctuary. Zach had been a little surprised earlier to find that so
many attended the midweek prayer meeting. It had been years
since he had done so himself, but he'd enjoyed the concen-
trated prayer that evening. Afterward, numerous individuals
had journeyed into the Annex on various missions, he and
Kylie among them—though she hadn't arrived, fresh from
the diner, until several minutes after the conclusion of the
prayer service.

From the office where Mrs. Ferber gave instruction,
Zach could see into the Fellowship Hall where Arabella and

Jasmine were separating a huge tub of flatware into various containers while the triplets, all girls not much more than four years old, industriously colored on sheets of paper. Zach had been disturbed to hear some weeks ago that Jasmine had become engaged to Samuel's grandson, Cade, Charley's boy. Much to Arabella's dismay, the young couple planned to marry in December. Zach wouldn't know Cade if he saw him, but it occurred to him that Kylie probably would.

He looked her way in speculation, receiving the slight arch of one slender brow and the barest curl of a smile in return. A cleared throat had them both staring at Mrs. Ferber again, but Zach couldn't help hiding a smile behind his hand, disguising it with a vigorous nose rub. They passed another half hour in that fashion, with Mrs. Ferber doing what she did best—teaching—and Zach and Kylie re-enacting their classroom days.

Arabella and the girls left before Mrs. Ferber finished, grinning and waving as they filed past the large interior windows of the office. Zach winked at each of the triplets, making them giggle. Mrs. Ferber made Kylie giggle when she called Zach on it.

"Still impressing the young ladies, I see, Mr. Clayton."

"My, um, cousins," he muttered, thoroughly chastised.

"I am aware," said Martha Ferber dryly. "Now, let's just go through this one more time, shall we?"

They went through it one more time. Afterward, Mrs. Ferber assigned them the time slot of Thursdays between 7:00 and 9:00 p.m., starting the very next night. Zach felt pleased. The phone hadn't rung since they'd been there, and he'd enjoyed even the silent interaction with Kylie. He could think of worse ways to spend his Thursday evenings than sitting in a small room with her.

Finally, they prepared to leave. When he thanked Mrs. Ferber for her time, she surprised him with a hug. "It's good to have you back, Zach Clayton. Your mama would be pleased."

He didn't know what to say to that. Had his mother missed him so much that she'd complained to her friends about his absence? He wished he'd spent more time with her after his father had died. Instead, he'd made phone calls and let his resentment toward his father keep him away. Now it was too late. Why hadn't he realized what he was doing before her death?

Zach and his dad had never gotten along, and matters had only gotten worse after little Lucy's death. George Jr. had been a chip off the old autocratic, demanding, overbearing block that was George Clayton, Sr., but without the drive or cunning. Zach had thought that he'd spared his mother the angst of their famous clashes. His dad's sudden death had left no chance ever to mend the rift. All of Clayton had then become a black hole of grief and regret in Zach's mind. He'd found every excuse to stay away after that, but he was beginning to understand now that Clayton could actually be *home* again.

His parents had both gone, but he still had real family here, after all—Brooke, Arabella and the girls and, by extension, Jasmine. The thought of Jasmine made Zach wonder again what Kylie knew about Cade. Mentally framing how he would bring up the subject, he escorted her out to the parking lot. Before he could speak, she surprised him with her intent to walk over to the Feed & Supply, where her parents would be waiting to give her a ride home.

"We've just got the one vehicle," she explained. "They were going to work on the books tonight while I was in training."

"What about tomorrow night?" Zach asked.

"I don't know. Guess I'll walk over here from the diner and Mom or Dad will pick me up later."

"I could give you a lift out to your place," Zach offered lightly.

"Oh, I don't want to put you out," she muttered, ducking her head.

Disappointed, Zach didn't push it. Instead, he said, "Well, let me drop you at the Feed & Supply tonight anyway."

She shrugged and moved toward his Jeep. "Okay."

As soon as she belted in, Zach started the engine and asked, "What can you tell me about Cade?"

"Cade Clayton?"

"Is there another Cade around here?"

"Not that I'm aware of. What do you want to know?"

Zach drove the vehicle across the parking lot and turned left on Flicker Avenue. "Anything. Everything."

"Well, he's a good kid. He's kept his nose clean. He's polite, bright, hardworking…"

Zach shot her a skeptical look. "We're talking about Charley's son, right?"

She tilted her head. "Charley's no prize. It's an open secret that he fakes a bad back to get out of work and collect disability, but no one's more ashamed of that than Cade. If anything, it's made Cade want to do better, and I believe he will."

Zach made another left on Hawk Street. "How so?"

"Cade's a vocal Christian, very popular and noted for his sincerity. He's my favorite out of the whole family, although I have no problem with his half-brother, Jack McCord, either." She shot him a look from the corners of her eyes. "Samuel's family, I mean."

Zach tried not to wonder just who her favorite might be on George's side of the family. "Go on."

"Well, let's see. Cade was a good student, and he works at anything he can find. Besides that, he's polite, respectful, helpful. He talks about going to college and wanting to be a doctor. And he's utterly devoted to Jasmine Turner."

"Yeah," Zach said sourly, downshifting to crawl over the train tracks just north of Railroad Street. "That's the problem." He braked and turned right into the graveled yard of the Feed & Supply. "Arabella is not happy about this so-called engagement."

"They *are* young to be getting married," Kylie remarked as they bumped across the yard toward the main building.

"Too young," Zach concurred, wondering why he felt the need to talk to her about this. He seemed to flap his gums compulsively around her. "The whole family is up in arms about it, frankly. From what Jasmine says, Samuel's side of the family is as upset as we are. Maybe more so."

"That's too bad," Kylie said. "Pull around back."

Rustic and unpretentious, the store itself stood dwarfed by the portable metal silos and prefab storage warehouse behind it. Zach followed directions, swinging the open Wrangler around the building.

"I just keep hoping they'll lose interest in each other and forget the whole thing," he told Kylie.

"Been known to happen," she commented wryly, cutting a glance at him from the corners of her eyes.

"At the last minute, even," Zach said with a chuckle, bringing the vehicle to a halt.

"The very last."

They both laughed, and she hopped out. He grinned at her through the open side of the uncovered Jeep. "See you tomorrow."

She waved and started toward the building. A light glowed in one corner window. Zach watched, the engine idling, until she opened a metal door and went inside. Smiling, Zach cut a wide loop in the yard, returning to Hawk Street, which dead-ended into Bluebird Lane. Less than three minutes later, Zach parked, then let himself into a dark, empty house.

Tomorrow, he thought, feeling lonely in a way that he didn't know how to explain, *can't come soon enough.*

"Hey, you," Erin said, greeting Zach as he came through the door into the diner on Thursday evening. Kylie noticed that he had changed out of his uniform—or what passed for a uniform with him—into jeans and a simple T-shirt of a royal blue so intense that it made his dark eyes seem even bluer than usual.

"Hey, yourself," he returned with a smile, taking in the other occupants of the café before striding toward the counter, which Kylie wiped with a cloth dipped in a vinegar and ammonia bath.

She tossed a nervous glance toward the table where Vincent sat with one of his cousins and a friend, laughing loudly. They'd come in ten or fifteen minutes earlier, demanding that Kylie serve them coffee. Since they'd obviously been drinking, Erin had immediately put on a fresh pot. When Kylie had served it, Vincent had ignored her. She knew that to be a petty form of punishment but had welcomed it nonetheless. Vincent's gaze now followed Zach avidly as he sank down on a stool directly in front of Kylie.

"I'm about finished here," she muttered, wringing out the cloth and hanging it on the edge of the sink behind her. She knew that look on Vincent's face. The sooner they got out of there, the better.

"Take your time," Zach said cheerfully. It seemed to her that his voice carried excessively well. "Thought I'd catch a plate of dinner before we go."

Kylie felt her chances of getting out of the diner without the eruption of a major scene plummet. Erin stepped in to offer a quick solution.

"We've got some pot roast left. I can side it with potatoes, carrots and peas, but the hot rolls are gone. All I can offer is a couple slices of white bread to go with it."

"Sounds great. Bring it on."

She turned to the kitchen pass-through window, calling out, "Dish up those leftovers, boys, and side it with a couple slices of lily white." Glancing at Kylie, she smiled and walked toward the cash register, saying, "Set him up with a cola, then you're done for tonight."

Kylie quickly filled a glass with ice and produced a bottle of Zach's favorite beverage.

"Thanks," he said, a relaxed smile on his handsome face. He smelled faintly of aftershave, and the smoothness of his jaw tempted Kylie to run her fingertips across his skin. "Why don't you come around and take a seat?"

She shot a glance at Vincent's table, aware of a deepening silence, but Zach's gaze never wavered. Gerald slid a plate onto the service ledge and slapped the "order up" bell. Kylie took the plate and set it before Zach.

"Come on," he said softly. "Keep me company while I eat, then we'll walk over together."

After a moment, she nodded and moved the length of the counter, slipping past Erin at the cash register. They exchanged loaded looks before Erin went back to organizing the cash drawer. Kylie sent up a silent prayer that Vincent would not start a fight.

Ignoring him as much as possible, Kylie walked around the end of the counter to the stool on the far side of Zach and climbed onto it. He picked up his fork, inhaled loudly and called out, "Most appetizing leftovers I've ever been served."

"Thanks," came a voice from the kitchen.

Zach dug in, humming his approval. Kylie knew that the dark, rich meat would literally fall apart in his mouth. He shoveled in several quick bites before Vincent suddenly appeared at his elbow. Zach never paused, just kept eating.

"You got a real taste for leftovers, don't you?" Vincent sneered. He shot a venomous glare at Kylie, adding, "My leftovers especially."

Zach frowned but did not look at Vincent. "Kylie is no one's leftovers."

Vincent ignored that. "You best get in line, lawman," he prodded loudly. "I hear every single man in the county is sniffing around her."

Kylie felt her cheeks heat and opened her mouth to say that her social life was none of Vincent's business, but Zach's hand landed heavily on her knee. She just barely managed not to jump, her tongue glued to the roof of her mouth.

"Is that so?" Zach asked conversationally.

Smirking at Kylie, Vincent named two men who worked with him at the mine. Each had asked Kylie out since she'd called off the wedding. She'd turned them down, sensing something not quite right about the invitations. Could Vincent have put them up to it? But why?

Zach took a bite of carrots, chewed and swallowed before turning his head to look at Vincent. "I've got a pretty good sniffer myself," he said calmly, "and it tells me that you've been drinking." Vincent backed up a step. "Folks can get arrested for drinking and causing trouble, you know. Am I going to have to arrest you, Vincent?"

"I'm not causing trouble," Vincent declared.

"No? I sure hope not, but see, I get to be the judge of that. As of yet, I'm undecided, but I have to tell you, I don't like the way you're talking about the lady. Now, why don't you sit down and leave us alone?"

Backing up another step, Vincent laughed. It came out as a harsh, mirthless sound that did not quite cover his nervousness. Though sober enough to realize that he might have made a misstep, Vincent remained too proud not to try to save face. Glancing at his buddies, he fixed his sneer and exclaimed, "She's not the sweet little thing you think she is."

Zach laid down his fork with great care and swiveled to the side. The tension instantly ratcheted up several notches. Quickly, Kylie grabbed the wrist of the hand on her knee in a silent plea. His shoulders heaved, but he kept his seat.

"I think you boys are ready to leave."

He turned his head and stabbed a dark look at the two snickering miscreants with Vincent. They both leapt to their feet.

Vincent reeled toward the door, snarling, "Suits me!" He threw a fulminous challenge at Erin. "Your coffee don't sit too well in my stomach. And neither does your clientele."

"What a shame," she chirped cheerfully. Les Clayton, Vincent's first cousin, reached into his pocket for money, but Erin waved him away. "On the house."

A tall, lanky fellow with thin, dark hair that hung in his narrow eyes, Les displayed little intelligence and a tendency to be easily led, like most of Vincent's running buddies. When not playing the willing stooge for Vincent, whom he hero-worshipped, Les worked at the grocery store for minimum wage. He followed Vincent and the other man toward the door.

"I hope you're walking," Zach told Les sternly.

"Yes, sir. I—I mean, no, sir. That is, I'm the designated driver because Vincent says I don't have a head for alcohol. Puts me right to sleep."

"You're wise to keep away from it," Zach rumbled.

The fellow bobbed his head and rushed out. Only when the door closed behind them did Zach turn back to his plate. Kylie managed to release her grip on him, and he slowly took his hand away from her knee, reaching for his drink.

"Well, that was interesting," Erin commented before going into the kitchen.

Kylie let out a silent sigh of relief. Beside her, Zach forked up a big bite of mushy, brown potatoes, but then he left it dangling there for a long moment.

"So," he said, "you're dating again."

Kylie's gaze jerked to the left, landing on his strong profile. "No, but I have been asked out."

Zach ate the potatoes and reached for a slice of bread. Folding it, he mopped up some of the thick, dark gravy. "You were asked, but you didn't accept."

"That's right."

Zach stuffed the bread into his mouth, but he couldn't hide that dimple in his cheek, the one that showed itself whenever he smiled. Was he pleased that she had turned down dates? Her heart speeding up just a little, Kylie decided to test that theory.

Hanging both elbows on the edge of the counter, she said smoothly, "I don't want to jump into another relationship too quickly."

His gaze dropped to his plate. Using his fork, he separated a chunk of meat from the mound on his plate. "Probably wise," he said and went on eating.

Kylie slumped a little. *Silly thing,* she scolded herself. *He's not interested in you. He's just ascertaining the facts. It's part of his job.*

Besides, he was right. She would undoubtedly be wise not to jump into another relationship too quickly. Very wise. And very…alone.

No, that was foolish. She was no more alone now than she'd ever been. She still had her family, even if Mariette would be going away to college soon.

Suddenly, life without her baby sister seemed oddly bleak. Who would keep her up half the night talking? Who would borrow her jeans and stain her tops, bounce on her bed in the mornings and confess innocent secrets? Who would compliment her and offer impulsive hugs? At least their parents would have to make fewer trips to town.

Zach pushed his now empty plate away and reached for a clean paper napkin to blot his mouth. "That was excellent. I'm ready to answer phones now. How about you?"

"I was ready ten minutes ago."

He chuckled, got up and walked around to the cash register to pay. Erin came out of the kitchen to take his money while Kylie fetched her handbag from the back room. She met him at the front door, and they set off into the night. They crossed the street to the green then walked a diagonal line toward the church. Halfway there, he spoke.

"Something's going on at the church tonight. Parking lot's almost full."

"Pizza supper for the youth group," she said. "Mariette's there. Dad dropped her off earlier."

"Where'd they get the pizzas?" Zach wondered.

"In the freezer section of the grocery store. They bake them in the fellowship hall kitchen."

"Ah."

"They'll be finished in another hour or so," she said. "Poor Dad, he'll have to run back in to get her and then come back after me later."

"My offer to drive you home after our shift stands."

"Really? You don't mind?"

Zach stopped and parked his hands at his waist. Kylie came to a halt a step or two later and turned to look at him inquiringly. "How many times you want me to make this offer, Kylie? Three? Four? Half a dozen?"

"I—I just don't want to take advantage of you, Zach."

"If I thought you would be taking advantage, I wouldn't have made the suggestion. Now, do you want the ride or not?"

"Yes. I do. Thank you."

He started toward the church again, muttering, "Maybe

those two men should have asked more than once. Is that how it goes with you? Never accept the first time?"

"No!" She hurried to catch up with him. "Why would you think that?"

He shrugged. "Vincent apparently asked you out for years before you agreed."

She rolled her eyes. "You know why that was! Besides, I'd have been better off if I'd never accepted a date with him. But we're not talking about dates. Are we?"

"Nope," he said, looking straight ahead.

She tried very hard not to wish that they were. And failed miserably.

Chapter Six

They fielded two calls on the help line in the first hour. One came from an elderly gentleman who needed a ride to the county Social Security office the following week. The other involved a local grade school boy being bullied by another student. Zach took down all pertinent information and promised to take care of it.

When he hung up, Kylie asked, "What are you going to do?"

"I'm going to arrange a visit for the pastor and me with that boy who is bullying and his dad. Then I'm going to speak to that mother and show her son a thing or two about sticking up for himself. And then I might just speak to the principal. He has a responsibility to control this sort of stuff."

Zach's solution seemed perfect to Kylie. They spent the rest of the time talking. She learned that, as suspected, Zach had little affection for uniforms and that he'd like his better if it came with a cowboy hat.

"A cowboy hat! You surely weren't wearing a cowboy hat down in Miami."

"No, I wasn't, but I've been known to wear a cowboy hat in the past. I grew up around here, after all. Been a long time, though. Too long."

"We've got some hats at the Feed & Supply." She chuckled, remembering the particular incident that had convinced her dad to stock a few hats in the store. "Keeps the local ranch hands from having to drive over the mountain if theirs accidentally winds up beneath the tires of a truck."

Talk moved from subject to subject. Kylie told Zach about her apprenticeship and how much she enjoyed planning weddings. They talked about their respective childhoods. Hers had been idyllic. His had been fun but stressed with discord. His parents' marriage hadn't been particularly happy, and Zach had often been at odds with his father.

"We didn't do many father-son things," Zach told her. "Dad was too wrapped up in his brother Vern and answering their father's beck and call. I guess that's one reason I was never close to my grandfather. I felt like he kept my dad and uncle on a string, which he yanked often. It interfered with…everything else. After Lucy's death, it all got worse. I couldn't be in the same room with my father without an argument erupting. So, I stayed away. Then he died."

They discussed the accident that had taken the lives of his father and uncle until Zach sighed and rubbed a hand over his face and head.

"I don't know why I'm telling you these things. I never tell anyone these things."

Kylie couldn't help smiling. "Well, I'm glad you've told me."

The happy cacophony of young voices told them that the youth meeting had broken up. Soon teenagers began filing past the office window in small groups.

Mariette came in to say hello. Kylie got up and went around the table to hug her sister. Kylie introduced Mariette to Zach then turned red when Mariette waggled her eyebrows and remarked, "He's a lot better looking than old Diggers."

Seeing that she'd embarrassed her sister, Mariette patted

Kylie's shoulder but made matters worse by declaring, "Of course, that's not saying much."

Zach snorted with barely suppressed laughter.

"Oh! I mean, well, Diggers is…not fat. Exactly. And you…" She waved a hand at Zach. "You're absolutely… Okay, I'm shutting up now."

Just then, Jasmine stuck her head in the door. "Mariette, your dad's out front. Hi, Zach."

"Hi, Jasmine."

"Thanks, Jas," Mariette said as the other girl disappeared again. Mariette smiled apologetically at Kylie. "Not a moment too soon, huh?"

"More like five minutes too late!" Kylie shot back, laughing.

"I'm sorry. Me and my big mouth." She grinned at Zach and said, "But he is cute."

"Just tell Dad that he doesn't have to come back into town tonight," Kylie instructed, taking her sister by the shoulders and turning her toward the door.

"How will you get home?" Mariette asked.

"I, uh, have a ride."

Mariette turned in the doorway and slid a speculative look over Zach, who smiled and said, "She has a ride."

"O-h-h-h." She winked. "Thanks."

"No, thank you," Zach said.

Mariette giggled, pulled a face at Kylie and bounced away. Kylie groaned.

"I'm sorry."

"Hey, no complaints. I'm the cute one. Cuter than Diggers, anyway."

Kylie laughed. "You certainly are. Cuter than Diggers, that is."

"Ouch."

Suddenly Jasmine returned—and not alone. "Zach, can I introduce you to someone?"

Zach slouched back in his chair. "Sure." He looked the young man with her up and down. "You must be Cade. You were a child last time I saw you."

Dark-blond hair and soulful brown eyes enhanced Cade's muscular build. "Yes, sir." Coming forward, he put out his hand with quiet, polite self-assurance. "Pleased to meet you."

Zach took his time leaning in and reaching out to clasp palms. Jasmine hurried to cover the awkward silence, saying shyly to Kylie, "I hope you don't mind me saying so, but I thought your wedding, that is, *almost* wedding, was just lovely."

Kylie couldn't help feeling pleased. "Why, thank you."

Tall and slender with long, straight, brown hair and vibrant blue eyes, Jasmine was a particularly striking girl. She quickly warmed to the subject of weddings. "The decorations you used were so beautiful. I would never have thought of making garlands from tree leaves and grasses."

"Well, when you don't have much money…" Kylie began.

"I know. That's why I was wondering…" Jasmine stepped closer, her hands twisting together. "Would you mind…" She cast a glance at Cade, who smiled and nodded encouragingly. "Do you think you could help me plan our wedding? It's scheduled for December, so we have some time. What we don't have is much money, but Mariette says you're a genius at figuring out ways to do things inexpensively. We could always elope, but I figure we're only going to do this once, you know? It ought to be as special as we can make it. I could really use some tips on how to do that."

"That sounds like fun," Kylie said, smiling.

"Hold on a minute," Zach said, rising slowly to his feet. "What does Arabella have to say about this?"

Jasmine faced him with perfect aplomb. "Arabella is very

stressed out right now, trying to keep the house going on her own since Grandpa George passed."

"That's not what I mean, and I think you know it," Zach said softly, folding his arms.

Jasmine shook her hands in a gesture of frustration. "She thinks I'm too young to be planning a wedding or anything else. Okay? But I'm not, and I'm going to prove it to her." Her gaze zipped back to Kylie. "You'll help me do that. Right?"

Kylie glanced at Zach. He frowned darkly, but planning a wedding didn't mean it would take place. She was walking proof of that fact. Besides, she didn't have the heart to turn down Jasmine's request. "I'll help you."

"Great!" Jasmine bounced on her toes and clapped her hands, ecstatic.

Beside her, Cade beamed, too. Kylie had noticed that whatever made Jasmine happy made Cade happy too. She hoped Zach could see that, but if he did, it didn't seem to matter.

"You two are bright enough to realize that marriage is tough in the best of circumstances," he lectured sourly.

"Yes, sir," Cade admitted. "But sometimes marriage is definitely the best option. At least that's how I read Scripture anyway."

"We've discussed our options," Jasmine said, reaching blindly for Cade's hand. His met hers unerringly, like two magnets unable to resist the pull of the other. "And marriage is our only alternative. We can't live with anything else."

"And won't settle for anything less," Cade added quietly.

Dropping his arms and shaking his head, Zach seemed as frustrated as Jasmine. "How do your father, grandfather and Jack feel about the engagement, Cade? I can't believe they're pleased."

"No one's pleased but us," Cade said, squeezing Jasmine's hand, "and no one's more unhappy about that than we are. But Jasmine and I know something that no one else can."

"Which is?" Zach demanded suspiciously.

Cade looked at Jasmine, and the love shining in his eyes made a lump rise in Kylie's throat. "That we belong together and that getting married is absolutely right for us. We'll just have to keep praying for hearts and minds to change."

Jasmine clasped his hand with both of hers, beaming. Kylie realized suddenly that she had never once looked at Vincent that way and that she never would have. These kids, she thought, had more going for them than she'd even imagined. Stepping forward, she placed a hand on Jasmine's shoulder.

"I'll put some ideas together, and we can talk in a few days."

"Oh, thank you!" Jasmine exclaimed, breaking free of Cade long enough to hug Kylie.

Smiling, Cade gave Zach a respectful nod before linking hands with Jasmine again. They left the room talking softly together.

Kylie waited until they passed out of sight before turning to Zach. "They're obviously in love."

"I can't fault their approach to this whole business," he grumbled. "At least they're honest, and they're obviously trying to be patient, but as for love…" He shook his head. "Who knows?"

"I guess you've never been in love then," Kylie heard herself say.

His gaze settled on her face, and for a long moment she couldn't seem to breathe. Finally, he murmured, "Thought I might be a time or two, but no." His gaze sharpened. "What about you?"

She had to be as honest as he had been. "Same. Seemed possible a few times but just never happened."

"Not even with Vincent?"

"No. I thought we'd established that fact."

"Mm. And I thought we'd concurred that Jasmine and Cade are too young for marriage."

"You don't like that I agreed to help them," Kylie surmised softly.

"I don't like anything about this."

"Has anyone seen Reverend West?"

Kylie's attention jerked to the doorway again. Darlene and Macy Perry stood there.

"He was supposed to sign a letter for me this evening," Darlene went on, "so I could drop it in the mail first thing tomorrow morning."

"Sorry, haven't seen him," Kylie said, shaking her head. "But the youth Bible study let out a little while ago. Maybe he's in the youth room."

"Okay. I'll have a look. Thanks." She glanced down at Macy, asking, "Want to wait here for me?" The young girl nodded shyly. Darlene looked to Kylie and then Zach. "Do you mind?"

"Not a bit," Kylie replied.

"It would be our pleasure," Zach said, smiling at the girl.

"I won't be a minute," Darlene promised, moving away. The woman looked too fragile to be standing upright, but she somehow managed to work most days in the church office.

Macy stood off to the side, nervously twirling a lock of blond hair around her finger as she looked over at Zach.

"So what have you been up to?" he asked, trying to break the ice.

"I'm helping Mama secretary," the girl replied solemnly. "She gets real tired, so I fold stuff and put on stamps and staple pages together, things like that. Sometimes she lets me play games on the computer."

"Cool."

"I'm lousy at typing," she confessed self-consciously.

"Me, too. I think you'll get better, though," Zach said.

"I think you will, too," she said.

"Not a chance." He held up his hands, waggling his fingers. "All thumbs."

Macy giggled, and Zach traded a look with Kylie, showing how pleased he was to make inroads with the beleaguered young girl.

"So your Mama's tired a lot, is she?"

The sparkle left her pretty blue eyes. "Yes. But I help, and the reverend says she can rest when she wants. It's a blessing of a job, Mama says."

"That's good."

She shuffled her feet. "So how come you're not wearing your sheriff shirt?" she asked, clearly anxious to change the subject.

"Needs washing," Zach said, glancing up at Kylie. She had to bite her lip to keep from chuckling aloud.

"Oh," Macy said, tentatively patting his shoulder. "I like this one."

"Me, too," Kylie had to say.

"Thanks," Zach said, smoothing a hand over his chest. "Blue's my favorite color. What's yours?"

"Hot pink!" she grinned, pointing to her plastic eyeglasses.

"What's yours?" Zach asked Kylie then.

"Hm. Turquoise."

"Yeah, that's good, too," Macy agreed. "I *really* like pink and turquoise together."

Again, Zach and Kylie traded amused glances. Darlene came back into the room a few moments later. "Found him. The reverend will take care of everything so we can sleep in tomorrow. Thanks, guys."

"You're welcome," Kylie said cheerfully.

Darlene held out a hand to her daughter, "Let's go, sweetie. Oh, and by the way, I've reset the locks for the evening. You'll be able to leave the building, but you won't be able to get back in."

"No problem," Zach said.

Macy ran around the table to take her mother's hand. "Bye!"

"Bye-bye."

"See ya."

Mother and daughter waved and went out.

Zach shook his head, remarking softly, "That's another troubling situation."

"Darlene's very ill, isn't she?"

Zach nodded. "Darlene has asked Brooke to take custody of Macy when the time comes that she can no longer take care of the girl on her own."

"Oh, wow. I didn't know it was *that* serious. Brooke's going to do it, of course."

"Of course. Macy is practically family already." He cocked his head, murmuring, "In fact, she looks so much like Brooke did as a little girl that she could almost *be* family."

"Isn't it funny how God works?" Kylie remarked. "What are the chances of that, do you suppose?"

"Slim," Zach answered with a ruminating frown. "About as slim as Jasmine and Cade making a successful marriage, I'd say."

Kylie bit her tongue. She hated being at odds with him. He was a kind, decent man, and he displayed a lot of good sense, but Kylie had begun to think that Jasmine and Cade had a better chance of making a life together than most couples. Still, she could understand the family's doubts.

What she couldn't understand was the sense of trepidation and sadness that she felt because of a simple difference of opinion about a matter that neither she nor Zach could control.

* * *

The fact that he could do nothing to change Jasmine's mind or the Perrys' situation irked Zach. Taking control of tricky situations and finding reasonable, effective solutions had become a habit with him. Unfortunately, these two cases stumped him. That didn't keep him from brooding on the matter, though.

While Kylie took down information provided by a concerned church member about a poor family apparently living out of a tent on public land, Zach worried about Jasmine and the Perrys. Even as he and Kylie signed out on the computer and left the now silent building, allowing the door to lock behind them, his thoughts remained troubled.

He should have been able to reason with Jasmine, but as long as she remained enthralled with Cade, he didn't expect her to listen. Zach couldn't quite dislike Cade now that he'd met the boy, but he couldn't quite trust him either. Even if Cade hadn't been one of Samuel's grandsons, he was still too young to be anyone's husband, just as Jasmine was too young to be anyone's wife. Unfortunately, Colorado law said they were old enough to make such decisions, and without the law to back him up, Zach felt powerless.

As for Darlene Perry's health, Zach felt totally out of his depth. He only had prayer to offer in that case. Macy's resemblance to Brooke bothered him on some level that he couldn't quite identify, but every time he drew near to crystallizing his thoughts on the matter, something held him back. He had the same problem when trying to think about what had happened in Miami.

He and Kylie walked out to the Wrangler. While he handed her up into the passenger seat, her gaze did not quite meet his, but Zach's preoccupation led him to assume that she felt uncomfortable with the windowless doors.

"Buckle in," he ordered mechanically, wondering why he couldn't quite think about Miami.

God knew that he'd told the story of what had happened often enough; department policy had made it mandatory. Once he'd fulfilled police and city requirements, however, the whole incident had fled his conscious mind. Almost. It hovered there, just on the edge of his thoughts, like a mosquito that buzzed around his head, out of sight, but there nonetheless. He dared not really "look" at it or anything that reminded him of it.

He realized suddenly that he'd walked around Miami like a blind man, not daring to see what was around him. Had he felt that leaving would allow him to see clearly again? Maybe it would, in time. Maybe that's what his recurring dreams meant. Maybe he could finally work his way toward conscious, rational thought about the shooting without his emotions overwhelming him.

He made his way to Waxwing Road.

"It's about two miles now," Kylie told him. He glanced at the odometer, nodding. Night quickly enveloped them, broken only by the beams of the headlamps. A few minutes later she said, "This is it."

He turned through a cattle guard and followed a graveled drive into the dusty yard of a sprawling log home. Warm yellow light lit the windows, and tall trees framed the setting. He glimpsed the shape of an old-fashioned barn in the middle distance and then a swath of silvery grass running like a broad river between the barn and the dark spires of the mountains. A lovely place, it was just the kind of home that he'd like to own one day.

The thought occurred to him that, if the conditions of Grandpa George's will were met, a place such as this would not be out of his reach. An unexpected excitement quickened. For the first time, the inheritance—a quarter-million dollars and five hundred acres for each of the heirs—actually meant something to Zach. Then he thought of Lucas, the one least likely to make the move back to Clayton.

It was no secret how passionately Lucas had resisted their grandfather's attempts to get him back to Colorado. Some of the family wondered if he had disappeared so he couldn't be pressed to return now, but no one really believed that. Something had gone wrong with Lucas. Otherwise, one of them would have heard from him by now. Zach's unease about the situation increased daily.

Lord, let him be safe, Zach silently prayed.

That prayer had become a mantra since Zach had returned to Clayton.

He brought the Jeep to a halt, and the instant the tires stopped rolling Kylie blurted, "Zach, don't be mad at me."

What? A moment passed before her meaning sunk in. Momentarily dumbfounded, he killed the engine and twisted in his seat to face her.

"I'm not *mad* at you."

"Look, I know you think they're too young," she said quickly, "and maybe they are."

"Jasmine and Cade, you mean."

Kylie released her safety belt, nodding. "The thing is, though, no one can keep them from getting married, so why shouldn't I give them the benefit of my expertise?"

"Kylie, I'm not angry with you."

"You're not?" she breathed.

"No."

"It's just that you've been so quiet. I thought maybe you were upset with me for agreeing to help with the wedding."

"I'm troubled, yes, but I'm not *mad.*"

"Oh." She relaxed back into her seat.

"I'll admit that I'd rather this wedding didn't take place,"

Zach went on. "I just think it's a bad decision on Jasmine's part."

"Would you feel so strongly about it if Cade wasn't Samuel's grandson?"

"You mean, am I prejudiced against Cade because of Samuel and Charley? Yeah, probably so. But for good reason." He ran a hand over the top of his head. "On the other hand, I have plenty of reasons to question my own judgment."

"Somehow I doubt that," Kylie said with wry skepticism.

"If you only knew," he muttered, recalling the nightmare from the night before. Maybe he couldn't think rationally about what had happened in Miami, but he certainly could dream about it. Last night, he'd awakened in the middle of the incident, watching in horror as it all unfolded again in slow motion. He'd jerked awake at the pivotal moment and sat bolt upright in bed, sweating profusely, his lungs pumping like bellows. Thankfully he hadn't cried out. "In fact, I dream about my mistakes," he heard himself say.

"Well, that stinks," Kylie said, smiling sympathetically. "I can't imagine that you've made more mistakes than I have, though."

Maybe not more mistakes, he thought, *just bigger ones.* He opened his mouth to tell her the truth of it, remembering just in time that he did not particularly want anyone else, especially her, to know.

"I dream about being a big wedding planner in Denver," she confessed, "and instead I'm stuck here in Clayton."

"This place has kind of grown on me," he said, surprised to hear himself say it.

"It's not the place to become famous for your fabulous ideas and unique sense of style," she told him dryly.

"Like making garlands out of tree leaves and grasses," he surmised, remembering what Jasmine had said.

"Hey, you work with what you've got. Actually it was

small tree branches, stripped of their bark and twisted into a kind of rope with grasses woven in to cover what the leaves didn't."

"That's certainly unique."

"And it was very pretty, too, if I do say so myself."

Impressed, Zach leaned sideways. "You know, you don't have to be in Denver to market that kind of idea. I see people selling how-to stuff on the Internet all the time."

She lifted her eyebrows. "I hadn't thought of that." She considered for a moment. "That just might work." Leaning closer, she smiled at him. "Thanks for the idea."

He should have replied to that, but he couldn't think of the appropriate words. He couldn't think of anything except the shape of her lips as she had spoken. She might have spoken again. He couldn't be sure. The thundering of his heart drowned out the sound of her voice, but he registered every other detail: the lemony smell of the long ponytail lying against her neck, the smoothness of her skin, the delicate flare of her nostrils, the width of her slender shoulders beneath his arm.

What? When had he put his arm around her? He pulled back, completely disoriented. What was happening?

He knew suddenly what he wanted to happen. "How about having dinner at my house tomorrow night? Uh, Brooke, Gabe and A.J. will be there, too."

Kylie's face clouded. "Oh, Zach, I'm sorry. I already have plans."

Reality smacked him in the head with a decided *clunk*.

"Right." He sat back in his seat and reached for the steering wheel with both hands. Plans. She had plans. A date. That's what she meant. She already had a date. Well, it had to happen sooner or later. "Another time," he managed, striving for a light tone.

"Sure," she said, opening the door. "I'd like that." He

nodded, but he couldn't quite make himself look at her. "Okay. Well…thanks for the ride."

"You bet."

"Good night," she murmured.

"G'night."

She swiveled and slid off her seat. He'd started the engine before her feet hit the ground.

She waved goodbye and he curtly nodded at her. Then he wheeled the Wrangler around, feeling like the world's biggest fool. When last he glanced into his rearview mirror before turning toward town, she still stood there in the soft red glow of his taillights, in front of that inviting log house that had first made him think of having a real home.

"Not likely," he reminded himself.

Any of the remaining three heirs—Vivienne, Mei or Lucas—could fail to fulfill the stipulations of the will. Even with Mei and Lucas's mom, Lisette, still living in town, Zach wasn't sure that Lucas would return. Besides, Zach would probably be moving on himself after his year here. To a new town and a new job. One that didn't require uniforms.

The thought did not please as it should have. Somehow, in a matter of days, he'd started to think of Clayton as home again. Just as he'd started to think of Kylie as…*almost his.*

That notion was even more stupid than almost kissing her. Again! He didn't need the kind of trouble that being with her would bring. Vincent hated him enough already. Besides, she'd as good as said that she had started seeing somebody else.

The idea opened a hole in him. Nevertheless, he would do everything in his power to stay away from her.

Chapter Seven

Gabe Wesson pulled up in front of Zach's office late on Monday afternoon at almost the same instant as Zach did. Sighing inwardly, Zach realized that his neighbor and future brother-in-law had not come on a social call. The job had been this way for days. Nonstop.

The action had started before five o'clock that morning. It was Friday when the dispatch office had called out every available deputy to assist with a manhunt when an inmate at the county jail went missing. The inmate had turned up in the mess hall kitchen an hour later, making himself breakfast. Since then, Zach had served three warrants, assisted in two arrests and helped dismantle a drug lab in other parts of the county. Today he'd been dispatched to transport a suspected arsonist arrested by the Forest Service. That had necessitated use of the county car.

Zach got out, listening to the door creak on the old heap. Gabe met him at the front bumper.

"What's up?"

"Well, Deputy, you told me that I ought to be documenting everything that happens out at the mine, so I'm here to file a report."

Zach led the way to the door. "What now?"

"Somebody let the air out of at least one tire on every vehicle at the site."

"Yours included?" While unlocking the door, he nodded toward the pickup truck with the mine logo on the doors.

"Yes. It's no more than a nuisance because we have a number of air pumps at our disposal, but I have a lot of unhappy employees who are going to be late to dinner tonight."

Zach opened the door and flipped on the lights, moving rapidly behind the counter. "Let me get the paperwork for you."

He went to the file cabinet for the forms while Gabe looked around the place from the other side of the front counter.

Gabe said, "Wow, big improvement here. This actually looks like a place of official business now instead of a rat's nest with a desk."

Zach smiled. "Here are the forms. You can fill them out at home and turn them in later."

"I'll do that," Gabe told him, taking the papers from Zach's hand. The Perrys came in as he left.

"Hi, Zach! Bye, Gabe!" Macy smiled, hurrying around the end of the counter to greet him.

"Hey, sweetie pie! How you doing?" He was tickled that she no longer seemed shy around him.

"Good."

While returning Darlene's greeting, Zach lifted Macy up to sit on the counter. "You're looking mighty pretty today."

She blushed. "Thank you. So are you."

"You think so?"

Darlene lifted a hand to cover her laughter as Zach batted his eyelashes and pretended to stroke the long hair that he didn't have. Macy snorted at his antics.

"I meant you're looking very handsome today. Except…" She lifted a hand to his jaw. "You could use a shave."

Zach put on a crestfallen expression, and Macy giggled. Just then, a childish face pressed against the front window and a young voice called out, "Macy! Macy!"

Swiveling around, Macy waved excitedly. "That's Lily. Mama, can I go out and see her? We'll stay right there by the window."

"Sure, honey. Go ahead."

Macy hopped down and ran outside to talk to her friend. Zach chuckled. He turned his smile on Darlene.

"Can I help you?"

"You already have. Macy just wanted to stop in and say hello. She's very taken with you."

"Yeah, I can tell," he quipped, nodding at the window, which framed two giggling little girls.

"No, really," Darlene insisted. "Your experience with two younger sisters shows." She leaned closer, adding, "and the badge doesn't hurt."

Zach laughed, then saw Macy do something with her hand that was so much like something that his sister Vivienne would do that he caught his breath. That kid had to be related to the Claytons somehow. Might one of Samuel's sons be her father? Zach looked to Darlene again, slipping into detective mode.

"You know, I've been wondering about Macy's dad."

Darlene startled, blinking. "What?"

"Does he help you with her at all?"

Darlene's face immediately shuttered. "No. No, he doesn't."

"Have you thought of going after him for child support?"

"No! That's not possible," she said tightly.

Zach wanted to ask if the man was married, but he didn't want to embarrass her. "I could talk to him, if you like, discreetly."

"No one can talk to him," she said. "He cannot be reached."

"You mean that no one knows where he is? I might be able to help locate him."

"I mean, he's…he cannot be reached." Before Zach could make another query, she began backing toward the door, saying, "Well, we really only had a minute. Macy just wanted to pop in. I have to get home and make dinner. Thanks for your time."

She was out the door before he could say "No problem."

Definitely a mystery there. If he had a name, he could look into it. He had ways of finding people, after all. Lucas came to mind, as he did so many times throughout the day.

Lord, let him be safe.

The prayer flowed through Zach's mind. This time he added another plea to it.

And bring him home.

Maybe Lucas wouldn't consider Clayton home, but Zach realized suddenly that he did; that didn't matter, though, as long as they found Lucas well. As a veterinarian with patients and clients who depended on him, Lucas would not just take off for no reason. Zach took out his cell phone and called the number of his old friend in Florida, but his buddy with the state police had nothing to report. Zach suggested a trace on any credit card accounts that Lucas might have and agreed to a formal missing persons report to make it happen. He'd resisted that idea at first, sure that Lucas was tied up in something personal and wouldn't appreciate interference, but Zach had come to the point where he had to do *something*. He felt only marginally better for having done so and again put the matter in God's hands.

His stomach rumbled. Glancing at the clock on the wall, he saw that the dinner hour had arrived, but he really did not want to go home and cook tonight. Brooke spent all of her time with Gabe, and while the happy couple always welcomed him at the table, watching them together made him feel more alone than ever.

Looking across the green to the Cowboy Café, Zach thought of Kylie. Maybe she wouldn't be working this evening. Since she'd turned down his dinner invitation, he'd done his best to avoid her. That hadn't been difficult. He'd been as busy as a spider at a fly convention these past few days. He hadn't even been able to make church yesterday. Miami hadn't been this busy! Still, he could have seen Kylie easily by stopping in the diner. He had intentionally resisted the lure, but with his stomach cuddling up to his backbone, he decided to risk it. He couldn't avoid Kylie forever, after all.

After locking up the office, he drove around the green to the café. He spotted Kylie the instant he came through the door. She saw him at the same time, and any hope that he might draw one of the other serving staff vanished when she waved and started forward, a bright smile on her face.

Something happened inside his chest. It felt as if his heart smiled and cracked open in the same instant. Ridiculous. Scary, even. Gulping, he headed for a seat at the nearest empty table, mindlessly returning the greetings of others in the building, diners and servers alike.

Kylie set a bottle of cola and a glass of ice in front of him a split second after his backside hit the chair. In an effort to keep the conversation as short and impersonal as possible, he immediately ordered a burger and fries, adding, "I'm starved tonight."

"Get that right out for you," she said, her braid swinging out behind her as she whirled away.

Aching with an odd yearning relief, Zach poured his drink and waited for the bubbles to subside before taking a sip. She dropped down onto the chair to his left mere seconds later. He found that he couldn't quite look at her.

"I haven't seen you lately," she said softly.

"Been busy. Real busy."

"Zach, I hope—"

The phone clipped to his belt rang at the same time that the radio on his hip crackled. He shot to his feet, lifting one to his ear and pushing a button on the other. "Clayton here."

The radio spat out a code call while a dispatcher rattled the same information into his ear. A bad auto accident in the west pass had put lives at stake, and Zach happened to be the closest official. He didn't have to be told that county resources would be taxed by this one. "There in ten," he reported. Pushing his chair back with his legs, he stepped away from the table. "Cancel the order," he told Kylie.

"But you have to eat," she protested, on her feet next to him. "I get off in a half-hour and I have the truck tonight. I'll drop the food by your house."

Rather than argue with her, he pulled his wallet from his back pocket. "Fine. Great. Key's under the flowerpot. Just leave the food in the fridge. Thanks." He thumbed bills into her palm. She caught his hand and squeezed it. Somehow, that lifted his spirits. Experience told him that he was going to need that small show of support.

The modest frame house on Bluebird Lane appeared dark when Kylie pulled up. A silver car sat in the drive, but she didn't see Zach's Jeep, so she left her truck on the side of the road and carried the container with his food up the walk and onto the porch. After knocking and waiting, she decided to let herself in.

The key was exactly where Zach had said it would be. She found the lights and turned them on, then took a moment to look around. The décor was outdated and the furniture somewhat worn, but the house felt solid and homey. Glimpsing the kitchen at the end of the hall, she carried the food container in that direction. Darkness shrouded the back of the hall, but a light had been left on over the stove.

Kylie sensed Zach in the atmosphere. She could see him standing over the sink or sitting at the island or burying his head in the old-fashioned refrigerator. Smiling to herself, she disassembled the burger, put the meat and veggies on separate plates and set them in the fridge, finding it sparsely stocked. Afterward, she left his change on the island and wandered back into the living room, but she couldn't make herself go to the door.

Lately, Kylie had been thinking about how dangerous law enforcement could be. As the days had slipped by and she'd hadn't seen Zach except coming and going from the deputy sheriff's office, she'd begun to fear for his safety. Add to that the solemn expression on his face when he'd left the diner so hurriedly earlier, and Kylie reasoned that she had cause for genuine concern on his behalf.

She wanted to be here when he came in, partly because she worried about him and partly because she felt uneasy about the way they had parted on Thursday. The emergency call had thwarted her attempt to discuss that with him at the diner earlier, and she didn't want to wait until next Thursday. This might be her best chance to talk to him in private.

Settling down at the island in the kitchen to wait, Kylie made herself comfortable. Her sister texted her a little later to ask where she was. Kylie replied that she had taken dinner to a friend and might be a while.

Mariette sent a one-word question. "Who?"

Kylie didn't answer. Instead, she entertained herself by playing a simple game on her cell phone. That eventually palled, and she set it aside to think.

Recalling what Zach had said about Clayton "growing on" him, she almost got up and left, but that seemed foolish. If she chose her friends from among those who couldn't wait to see Clayton in their rearview mirrors, the pickings would be slim indeed.

Before long, she found herself in prayer. She asked for God's guidance and His blessings on those she loved. For her parents, she requested financial relief. She pleaded for Mariette to find success at college. After mentioning her boss, Erin, who might be the most overworked person Kylie knew, she went on to several members of the church, including the Perrys and a number of elderly individuals with failing health. Finally, she came to Zach, and as soon as she whispered his name, she knew that she'd been dancing around what lay heaviest on her heart.

"Just keep him safe," she said, "and give him rest. He looked tired tonight, and he missed his dinner, and only You know what he's dealing with right now." *Or what I'm doing here,* she added silently.

That was the crux of her disquiet. She didn't need to be getting involved with any man right now but certainly not with Vincent's cousin, however distant, especially if he truly meant to make home permanently here in Clayton. Yet, here she sat, unable to make herself go until she knew that he was well.

She heard a vehicle pull into the drive a few minutes later. Just seconds after that, a key slid into the door lock. Rising, she went to stand in the inner doorway of a small mudroom just as Zach stepped up into it, his every movement bespeaking exhaustion.

Seeing her, he blinked wearily and said, "Didn't expect to see you here."

"Come sit down. I'll heat up your dinner."

"Thanks. Let me take care of these boots, and I'll be right there."

He dropped down onto a narrow bench and crossed one leg over the other. Mud caked his boots, which smelled of gasoline. Kylie hurried into the kitchen, took the food from the refrigerator and went about heating the burger and fries in the microwave. While she did that, he took the boots outside, for airing, she assumed. Returning to the house, he came into the kitchen in his stocking feet and washed his hands at the sink.

"You didn't have to hang around here," he said, drying his hands on a plaid towel.

She shrugged and set the reassembled burger and hot fries on the island. He pulled out a chair.

"Didn't have anything better to do," she told him. "Hope the fries aren't too soggy."

"That doesn't matter," he said, sitting.

She turned to the refrigerator for condiments and placed those within his reach. He didn't wait. He'd already bitten off as much as he could chew. While he ate that first bite, he dressed the remainder of the burger with mustard and squirted catsup onto the plate.

She took down a heavy tumbler, dropped a few ice cubes into it from a tray in the freezer section of the refrigerator and filled the glass with water from the tap. Half the burger had vanished by the time she carried the water back to the island. Suddenly, he dropped the half-eaten burger onto the plate and shoved it away, dropping his head into hands.

"Zach?" Kylie swiftly skirted the island and laid a hand on his back.

He sucked in a deep breath, rubbed his hands over his face and lifted his head. "A man died tonight."

"Oh, no. Who?"

Zach shook his head. "I don't even know his name. He was a few years older than me. A big SUV knocked his little pickup right over the edge of the mountain, but no one even realized it until the driver of the SUV roused enough to tell us. It was a mess, five cars in total. The guy was conscious, but all I could do was hold his hand and pray with him while the rescue squad worked to get him out. He thanked me just before he passed. They tried to bring him back, but it was too late."

"That's so sad." Blinking back tears, she slid an arm across Zach's shoulders in a kind of sideways hug. "What a wonderful thing that was for you to do. I know it was tough, but that kind of ministry takes a special person."

He looked up at her with brows drawn. "I wouldn't call my work a ministry."

"But it so obviously is. Everything I've seen you do since you've been here proves that."

Smiling wanly, he lifted an arm and curled it about her waist, saying, "I never thought of it that way, but I have to admit that it's different here. It's not just about ferreting out the bad guys after the fact. That in itself is important, I know, very much so. But here at least sometimes I have the chance to stop things before they happen. I never realized how rewarding that could be." He rubbed his free hand across his forehead. "Maybe that's why I'm liking it here so much. I mean, despite past history and the everyday irritation of Pauley, this feels right for me."

Kylie knew a keen sense of disappointment at that statement, but she said only, "I'm glad." And she was, for him. She told herself that she didn't figure into it, but then he reached around her and pulled out the chair next to him.

"Me too. But it brought back painful memories. Can you sit with me a minute?"

"Of course." She tugged the chair around and sat, her knees just touching the seat of his chair. Leaning forward, she laid her forearms atop her thighs and prepared to listen.

"That man tonight was not the first one I've seen die. I lost my partner recently."

She couldn't let that pass without offering some sort of

comfort. Reaching up, she stroked the back of his head and neck. "What happened?"

He bowed his head, and she could tell that this was difficult for him, but he said, "It was a turf war gone bad. One drug dealer had taken another drug dealer hostage and was torturing him to find out where he'd stashed stolen drugs. My partner, Dave, and I stumbled into it while investigating a home invasion murder. There was no time to call for backup, but we pretended that we had and talked the perpetrator into giving up, because he happened to be alone." Zach paused and shook his head. "He'd sent his lieutenant, who was the guy we were after, for beer. Can you imagine?"

"No, I can't," she told him gently. "Go on."

"It was all over. The perp was facedown on the floor, and my partner was cuffing him. I went to check the so-called victim. He was a bloody mess and literally sobbing in relief, but the instant that his hands were free, he grabbed my gun out of my holster and tried to shoot his tormentor." Zach closed his eyes, whispering, "He hit my partner instead."

"Oh, Zach. I'm so sorry."

"The torturer jumped up and ran," he went on mechanically. "His victim managed to hit him in the leg before I got the gun away from him." Zach turned agonized eyes to her then. "I managed to save the life of a drug dealer and torturer, but my own partner…" Choking up, he looked away. "D-Dave was hit in the throat. Got his jugular. He bled to death in my arms." He smacked his knee with one fist. "A good man died that day because of me!"

She wrapped her arms around him. She couldn't think of anything else to do. "It wasn't your fault. It was not your fault."

He turned his head away, but his hands came up to curl around her arm where it passed across his chest. "That's what everyone else said, but it was *my gun*."

"You were trying to help an injured man."

"Bent on revenge," he pointed out bitterly.

"How could you know that?' she asked. "He was injured, crying. And what kind of man tries to shoot another man in front of two cops?"

He let out a watery chuckle. "There is that."

"I assume he's in prison."

"All three of them, the shooter, the torturer and the guy we came to question about the home invasion."

"That's good. Think of all the people they can't hurt now."

He sighed heavily. "That's what Dave's father said to me."

"I'm glad he could take comfort in that," she said softly. "Was Dave married?"

"No. He was dating someone, though, and I think they were getting serious. Guys don't talk much about that kind of thing. Guys don't talk much at all about anything that matters, really."

She laid her forehead against his shoulder, nodding. "I know."

Zach cupped her face then, lifting it so that he could look into her eyes. "Except to the women in their lives. I think that's why God gave us women because He knew that otherwise we'd all just clam up about what was bothering us, hold it inside until we exploded."

"Consider me your safety valve," she said, breathlessness robbing her voice of its intended humor.

He twisted slightly and his hands dropped to cup her shoulders. Wondering if he was going to move her away from him or kiss her, Kylie held her breath.

He kissed her.

Tilting his head, he slowly brought his lips to hers, giving her every opportunity to stop him. Instead, she tightened her hold, bringing him closer. Even as she mentally screamed at herself that falling in love with Zach might mean never getting out of Clayton, she thrilled to his kiss.

Vincent had never made her feel like this. No one had ever made her feel like this. She wondered if anyone else ever *could* make her feel like this.

The sound of the front door opening broke the kiss, but only when Zach whispered "Brooke" did Kylie think to pull away. She shoved her chair to one side and rose just as Zach's sister came into the room. He pulled his plate forward but didn't pick up the burger again. Instead, he twisted in his chair and smiled tiredly at Brooke.

"Sis."

"Hi." Brooke spread a curious look over the scene, smiling. "Hi, Kylie."

"Hello."

"I had to run out of the diner earlier without eating," Zach explained. "Kylie brought my food over." He looked at her then and said, "Thanks."

"My pleasure. And about what happened on the mountain tonight, I meant what I said. You performed a real ministry out there."

"What happened?" Brooke asked.

Before Zach could tell her, Kylie excused herself, saying, "I'll let myself out."

He looked like he wanted to argue, but Brooke sat down next to him. "What happened, Zach?"

He sighed. "I really ought to tell you. Everything."

Kylie slipped away. She couldn't help smiling as she went out to the truck, but as she drove home, she reminded herself again that falling in love with Zach would likely mean staying in Clayton from now on. She'd tried to settle for that once, and it had been a mistake. She promised herself that she wouldn't make the same mistake again, and then she prayed that it wasn't already too late.

Chapter Eight

"Sorry I'm late!" Kylie called, pushing through the front door of the Cowboy Café. She'd called earlier, but she felt compelled to explain again as she hurriedly crossed the room. "Something went wrong with the truck, and we had to borrow a car. A two-seater. For the four of us. But beggars can't be choosers, as they say, and at least we're all where we need to be now."

This monologue did not elicit the response that she expected, but she didn't take the time to wonder why. Instead, she stashed her small purse in the closet just inside the kitchen and went to take a pad and pencil from beneath the cash register. That's when she saw Zach sitting midway along the counter, his hands templed over a nearly empty plate of bacon and eggs. Her heart leapt at the sight of him. Smiling, she jammed the order pad into a hip pocket with one hand and slid the pencil behind her right ear with the other. When she moved toward him, however, Erin stepped into her path, a large vase of flowers in her hands.

"These came ten minutes ago. Glenda brought them over from the flower shop. Said she found an envelope when she opened up this morning. It had money, an order and a note for you in it."

"For me?" Kylie asked stupidly, blinking.

"Flowers and note. For you," Erin confirmed.

Kylie drew back in confused surprise even as Erin thrust the vase into her hands. Filled with a colorful variety of showy blossoms, including at least half a dozen pink roses, it held a small envelope pinned to a pink bow. Her name had been written on the outside. Puzzled, Kylie couldn't do anything more than stare at the arrangement for a long moment.

"Well, read the note," Erin urged. "We're all dying of curiosity."

Flustered, Kylie set the vase on the counter and looked around the room. Diners, mostly men, occupied a pair of tables, but two women sat at the counter. One of them, Janey Guilder, Kylie recognized from the Independence Day picnic. Janey smiled and nodded toward the flowers as if inviting Kylie to enjoy her surprise. Turning her attention back to the flower arrangement, she unpinned the little envelope. Extracting the folded paper, she silently read the sentiment penned in an unfamiliar hand. "Beautiful flowers for a beautiful woman. XOXO"

She turned the paper over in her hand but found it unsigned. Who on earth could have sent these? Other than her family, she couldn't think of anyone who might have been moved to send her flowers, and a family member would almost certainly have signed the note. Suddenly she thought of someone with whom she'd recently shared a heartrending moment. A smile curled her lips. Was this Zach's way of thanking her for last night? What an unexpectedly sweet thing to do!

She turned her gaze on him. Everyone else did, too. Obviously feeling the weight of that, he glanced around then declared, "Don't look at me."

Kylie felt a crushing sense of disappointment followed by utter confusion.

"So who's it from?" Jerome shouted from the kitchen, placing a plate on the pass-through shelf.

Frowning, Kylie looked at the card again. "I don't know. It's not signed."

Erin peeked over her shoulder and read the card. "Mmm-mmm. 'For a beautiful woman.' Well, you impressed someone." She gave Kylie a congratulatory pat and went to pick up the plate and deliver it.

Kylie glanced at Zach as one of several men crowded around a table called out, "Must be *another* one of her boyfriends."

Kylie felt her heart drop as a careful blankness came over Zach's face. He didn't scowl or frown or even smile, but she felt as if he closed himself off. Suddenly Kylie realized that she had never explained why she hadn't been able to go to dinner with him that night. She'd been mentally kicking herself for handling his invitation in such a clumsy fashion, but he had caught her off guard and, although she wouldn't have disappointed her sister for anything and their time together was dwindling away, a nail-polishing party had seemed like a pitiful excuse for turning him down, so she'd said nothing at the time. Now, he must think that she was seeing someone else. But she wasn't!

She wracked her brain for an explanation for the flowers, and a new thought occurred to her. She and Jasmine had recently put their heads together and discussed some ideas for the younger woman's wedding that had left Jasmine ecstatic.

"It must be Jasmine! A thank-you for my work as her wedding planner."

Zach's face went from blank to stony. Tossing aside his napkin, he rose from the stool. Frustrated, Kylie started toward him only to feel a hand on her forearm. She looked down to find Janey Guilder clasping her arm.

"Really? You plan weddings?" the young woman asked, leaning across the counter.

"Uh, yes. That is, sometimes."

"That's wonderful! I could certainly use some help planning my wedding. I could pay you, if you're interested."

Kylie blinked at her. Had she just heard correctly? Another client had just dropped in her lap? A *paying* client? *Now?* She flashed a wan smile in the other woman's direction.

"Th-that sounds great. Just give me a minute, will you?"

She looked toward Zach's seat, only to find it vacant. Turning her head, she saw him at the door, but before she could call out to him, he opened that door and walked through it, pulling it shut behind him. Kylie stared at that closed door for a long minute, vaguely aware of Janey chattering happily to the friend beside her.

Swallowing her hurt and disappointment, Kylie told herself this was for the best. She didn't know who had sent those flowers. It had to be some sort of mistake. At the very least, the note had been meant for some other woman. Nevertheless, if a simple vase of flowers had been enough to turn Zach away from her, well, then so be it. He could not be the guy for her, anyway, not if he really meant to stay in Clayton.

That did not make her feel one bit better, of course.

She had to force herself to turn and focus on Janey. When she did, she saw something that caught her attention. Janey had tied a colorful scarf about her throat. Patterned in rich shades of navy and green, it perfectly complimented the grass-green sleeveless top that she wore. But below the edge of that jaunty scarf, just above her collarbone, a bruise peeked out. The size and shape of a fingertip, that bruise made Kylie wonder if someone had put his hand around Janey's throat and tried to choke her.

Catching the other woman's gaze, Kylie leaned across the counter and quietly asked, "Are you okay?"

Frowning, Janey sat back and tugged on the knot of her scarf, using the sweeping end of it to cover the dark mark. "I don't know what you mean."

Kylie got the message loud and clear. Whatever had happened to put that bruise there, Janey would not talk about it. Did Rob Crenshaw have anything to do with that bruise? If he did, Janey would not admit it. All Kylie could do was smile and pretend that it didn't matter.

She'd gotten a lot of practice at that lately.

"Well, what did you expect?" Zach muttered to himself as he strode swiftly across the green.

A woman as lovely as Kylie would naturally have any number of men interested in her. Just because he'd kissed her didn't mean that she would suddenly turn everyone else away. He already knew that she'd been asked out. She'd admitted it after Vincent had brought it up. Then the other night she'd as good as told him that she had a date with someone else. Had she seen someone last night after leaving him?

He didn't want to think it, not after that kiss, not after he'd found her there in his house waiting for him. Having her there had awakened a need that he had managed to sublimate for a long time. In the past, he'd considered it unfair, given his occupation, to bring a wife and family into his life. Dave's death had made him rethink that, though. When Dave's father had made it clear that he regretted the fact that Dave had not married, Zach had realized that not only had his friend missed out on something important, some woman had missed out on being loved by a great guy. And now it was too late.

Zach didn't want to miss out. He wanted to come home every night to a woman who would share his burdens and soothe his disquiet. Someone who saw his work through the nobility of ministry and trusted him to do the right, best thing. Someone to whom he felt comfortable talking.

Someone who loved him and only him.

Maybe that woman would not be Kylie. She didn't want to live in Clayton, and he increasingly did. Okay, he could talk to her. In fact, he couldn't seem to stop talking to her, but that didn't mean they should be together. Maybe God had someone else picked out for him. Zach couldn't quite envision anyone else in that role at the moment, but God knew best, and if a woman did wait out there for him, well, he wanted her.

"Bring her on," he told God. "I'm ready whenever You are." A sour feeling in the pit of his stomach belied that sentiment, so he amended it to, "Make me ready to receive Your will, Lord, whatever it may be."

Pulling his keys from the front pocket of his jeans, he stepped up to the door of his office and began opening up the place. Catching movement from the corner of his eye, he turned his head and spotted Kylie's father coming toward him. Zach shifted around and put out his hand.

"Mr. Jones."

"Call me Gene," the older man said, glancing around as he gripped Zach's hand. "Can we go inside? I don't want Kylie to see me."

Zach's eyebrows rose. "Okay." Opening the door, he led the other man inside and went to lean against the counter, propping his forearms on the top edge of it. "What can I do for you?"

Gene Jones swept off his "gimme cap" and sighed. "This morning when I went out to start up the truck, someone had vandalized the interior. It's mostly cosmetic, I think. Ketchup, syrup, mustard and some sort of hot sauce all over everything. I was afraid at first that they'd poured it on the engine and in the gas tank, too, but it started just fine. The seats are cloth, though, so you can imagine what it's like. A real mess."

Zach shifted. "When do you think this happened?"

"Don't know. Sometime after ten because that's about when Kylie came home last night."

Ten. Kylie had left Zach's house around then, so whoever Kylie's secret admirer was, she hadn't seen him last night. For some reason, that made Zach feel a bit better.

"The wife wants to tackle the seats with a little steam cleaner she has," Jones said, "but I thought we ought to wait in case you wanted to take a look at it. The thing is, I don't want Kylie to see it like this. I just told her it was out of commission, but if she sees the vandalism, she's apt to blame herself."

"In other words, you think Vincent's behind this?"

"Who else?" Jones groused.

"It couldn't be some high school kids or an unhappy customer?"

"Not a customer, no, and what reason would anyone else have for doing something like this?"

Zach shook his head, then reached behind the counter and pulled out a report form, which he passed to Gene. "You can fill this out for the record and get it back to me. Now, let's go take a look."

Ten minutes later, they pulled up in front of the Jones house. The place looked as beautiful in the daylight as it had at night. Surrounded by trees, it sprawled in all its log splendor against the backdrop of the mountains. The barn that Zach had glimpsed in the night stood like a silver sentinel between the house and the mountain, its weathered wood and tin roof glinting in the sunshine. The dirty white truck sat at the apex of the broad drive in front of the house.

Parking beside it, Zach got out. Gene explained that the windows had been smeared with the same nasty gunk covering the seats, dash and floor, but Gene had cleaned them right away so his daughters wouldn't see the destruction. He'd then called a friend, who'd brought him an old, partially restored, two-seater sports car to drive. Zach looked the truck over and made careful note of the damage, but in the end the worst of it appeared cosmetic, just as Gene had expected. Zach would talk to Vincent but didn't expect to find out anything helpful. At least he could give Gene a report for his insurance company and help him clean up the mess. Gene opted not to file a claim because his deductible would be too high to make it worthwhile. He decided to use an old blanket to cover the seat so he could drive the truck back to the Feed & Supply where he could take his time cleaning it up.

Knowing that Vincent worked at the city maintenance yard, Zach drove over there, but the trip proved as useless for Gene Jones' purpose as Zach had feared it would. Vincent swore that he'd been with some of his buddies the previous night, and two of his coworkers backed him up on that. One of them even claimed to be bunking at Vincent's house and so had twenty-four-hour knowledge of Vincent's whereabouts. Zach recognized the other guy from the diner that morning. He'd made that wisecrack about the flowers having come from "another" of Kylie's boyfriends. That statement implied that *he,* Zach, could be counted among Kylie's boyfriends, and that notion had to come from Vincent. Things started to make sense.

No doubt Vincent, who lived just up the road from Zach's place, had seen Kylie's truck parked outside the house last night and come to the conclusion that she and Zach were seeing each other. That might account for both the vandalism of the truck and the flower delivery that morning. Could Vincent be trying to convince Zach that Kylie was playing the field, so to speak, or did he mean to punish Kylie for seeing Zach? Probably both.

After checking in by phone with the central office, Zach dropped by his house to change his uniform shirt for an old one that he kept for dirty jobs. He took a fresh uniform shirt on a hanger and drove over to the Feed & Supply. Gene could not have been more glad to see him, even though the report on Vincent disappointed them both.

They set to work, scraping off, wiping down, mopping up. When they had cleaned the handy interior surfaces, they removed the seats and floor mats to clean the crevices and creases. Then Gene set to steam-cleaning the seats. By the time they got everything put back together, the truck looked almost new, on the inside anyway. Gene decided to wash the outside, so Zach pitched in with that. While they scrubbed, they talked, and eventually the subject of the ranch came up.

"So where is this place of yours and Samuel's?" Zach asked, pausing to wipe his brow.

"Well, it's just north of my place," Gene said. The more he talked, the more Zach understood Samuel's thought process.

The six hundred and fifty acres, an odd-size parcel, stretched between the Jones' place and the three-thousand-acre spread that George Sr. had managed to put together around Great-Grandpa Jim's original mine site. With Gene's forty acres thrown in and the one hundred and eighty acres to Gene's south, which he said were under bank repossession, Samuel could reasonably expect to get his hands on nearly four thousand acres for a very minimal investment. He could just sit back and wait for Gene to default on his investment loan and George Sr.'s heirs to fail to fulfill the stipulations of the will. Then he could waltz in with a few thousand dollars and wind up the biggest landowner in the county. The plan was brilliant and diabolical. Zach couldn't let him get away with it, but he saved that topic for discussion with his sisters and cousins later.

By the time they were done, the sun had reached its zenith and dropped halfway to the horizon. "You've been a big help here, son," Gene said, coming to slap Zach on the shoulder.

"No problem."

"Come on inside."

Curious, Zach allowed himself to be steered into the building.

They walked through a short hallway, flanked on one side by a neat but crowded office and on the other by a neat but crowded storeroom, then between two long, low glass display cases. The interior of the store offered a mishmash of apparel, tools, leather goods, novelties, seed packets, wheelbarrows and any number of items that Zach couldn't identify offhand. Lynette Jones sat at a desk placed in a corner below two huge whiteboards with the quantities and prices of various bulk feeds written in red and black markers. While talking to someone on the phone, she typed figures into a computer. After ending the call, she rubbed out the quantity figure available for purchase on the whiteboard and wrote in a new number.

Zach, meanwhile, gravitated toward a display of straw and felt cowboy hats. Choosing an attractive tan felt, he checked it for size, price and weight. "You like that?" Mariette asked, appearing suddenly at his side.

"Good hat for the price," he said, putting it back.

"We've got some better deals," she told him, showing him a heavier felt. "Our customers just want work hats mostly. Can't hardly give these away."

Zach was impressed, but before he could try on the hat, her mother sauntered over. "How much do we owe you, hon? You put in nearly a full day's work for us. The least we can do is pay you."

"Oh, no, ma'am," Zach refused, shaking his head. "Today cost me nothing."

"Maybe he'd rather have a hat," Mariette suggested, bouncing on her toes.

"No, no, I couldn't—"

"Be doing us a favor," Gene interrupted. "Those things

have been sitting there taking up valuable space for months. I'm ready to let Kylie pass them out at the diner."

"We even put some up on that online auction site," Lynette said, "but by the time we shipped the things, we were losing money."

"Easier just to give them away," Gene muttered.

"And I know for a fact that you want one," Kylie said. Zach turned to find her standing behind him. His stupid heart did a double backflip at the smile on her face. "Go on. Try one on."

Zach delayed for a moment, trying to talk himself out of it, but then he picked out the right size and fit it to his head.

"You've worn a hat before," Mariette concluded. "Try just a little bit taller crown."

Zach acquiesced, allowing her to pull out hats for him to try.

"Oh, that's the one," Kylie said when he put the third hat on his head.

Doing his best to sound casual, he murmured, "You think?"

He watched in the mirror as the sisters looked at each other and said as one, "That's it."

"I'll take it," Zach decided. He tried to pay, but the Joneses wouldn't hear of it until he warned that such a gift could be seen as a bribe. Finally, they agreed on a very good price, leaving Zach the proud new owner of a buckskin-tan, 30X-weight, beaver-felt hat with a four-inch brim and a four-and-a-half-inch cattleman crown.

He was about to take his hat and go show it off to his sister when Lynette remembered that a package had come in the mail for Kylie. The latter looked at Zach and said, "I didn't order anything."

Before he could think better of it, he heard himself drawling, "Must be your secret admirer again."

"What secret admirer?" Mariette demanded, avid for every detail.

Kylie reluctantly explained as she opened the padded envelope. It bore no return address but did have a Clayton postmark. She shook out a small box wrapped in pink paper. Eying the thing as if it were a snake, she carefully pulled away the bow and peeled back the paper, then lifted the top from the box. A turquoise brooch nestled against a white velvet lining. A card tucked into the lid of the box read, "A beautiful jewel for a beautiful woman. Thanks for the other night. XOXO."

Kylie dropped the whole thing as if it had burned her fingers. "This is *not* from Jasmine," she declared as the brooch clattered against the glass top of the display case. "The flowers might have been but not this."

"What's it mean by 'the other night'?" Mariette asked, wrinkling her nose.

Kylie hugged herself. "I don't know. I spent my one night off last week with you, if you recall, and I sat down with Jasmine for a couple hours Saturday between shifts at the diner. Other than that, I haven't seen anyone."

"Except me," Zach said.

"Except you," she agreed quietly, holding his gaze.

Zach nodded, the knot in chest loosening. "Must be Vincent."

"But why?" Kylie wanted to know.

"Maybe he thinks he's turning potential suitors away by making it look like you're already dating someone," Lynette suggested.

"Makes sense," Gene said, "but what about the truck?"

"What about the truck?" Kylie demanded. That necessitated an explanation of the vandalism.

"Vincent must've seen the truck parked outside of Zach's house," she deduced. "His place is just up the road, after all."

Zach had come to the same conclusion, but he felt duty bound to point out that Vincent had an alibi. As usual.

"I'll bet he does," Lynette fumed. "Just like his grandpa taught him."

"Now, sugar baby…" Gene admonished.

"I'm not judging," Kylie's mom insisted. "I just know what I know."

Mariette picked up the brooch and examined it. "I've seen pins like this one next door at the flower and gift shop."

Kylie took the brooch, looked at Zach and said, "Come on." She took off without waiting for a reply. Zach nodded apologetically at her parents and hurried after her.

"I'll do the talking," he said as they strode across the graveled lot to the shop next door.

"Fine."

But the point proved moot. The proprietor agreed that the brooch resembled other pieces of jewelry for sale in her shop, but she flatly denied having sold anything to Vincent Clayton. She didn't know who had ordered the flowers, and the only pin she'd sold had been to old Mrs. Rader.

"Sherilyn's grandmother," Kylie pointed out needlessly as soon as she and Zach left the building.

"I doubt it would do any good to talk to her," Zach said. "Her mind's none too sharp so far as I can tell."

"But she's a link to Vincent."

Zach clapped a hand to the back of his neck, shaking his head. "I doubt that would convince the sheriff. It's not like anyone's been harmed, after all."

"So Vincent's going to get away with this?" Kylie demanded.

Zach sighed. "For the time being, I suppose he is, but I've put him on notice. He knows I'm watching."

"He'll just get others to do his dirty work," she scoffed.

Unfortunately, Vincent probably would do exactly that,

but until something more concrete turned up, Zach's hands were tied. Suspicion and probability with a single tenuous connection through a doddering old woman did not add up to an actionable offense. Unfortunately, that did not reduce the potential for more trouble if he let himself fall in love with Kylie Jeanne Jones.

Chapter Nine

The measure of Zach's determination to put some distance between himself and Kylie could be found in the fact that he considered staying home from church on Sunday. He'd kicked around the idea of begging off his shift at the help line on Thursday for the same reason. His sense of duty wouldn't allow him to shirk his responsibilities, however. Fortunately, duty had called him away on Thursday evening within the first half hour of the shift. A fire on the mountain had prompted the fire brigade to ask for roads to be closed, which had sent Zach barreling off with lights flashing.

Kylie and he had not been in the same building at the same time since. At least keeping his distance had apparently kept Vincent from harassing her—and Zach from making a fool of himself. Both reasons seemed to be legitimate excuses to stay home from church. One glance at the hat hanging on a hook on the closet door illustrated the fallacy behind such excuses, however.

He prized his new hat. He felt like a new Zach every time he put it on. Miami and all that had happened there felt part of the distant past when Deputy Sheriff Zach Clayton put on his hat. He even slept better lately, his dreams of Miami replaced by nebulous, indefinite vignettes, which he quickly forgot. He felt as if he donned all of Colorado and its history when he fit that buckskin beaver to his head. But he never put on the hat without being reminded of Kylie.

He never drove past Waxwing Road without thinking of her. He never looked through his office window without daydreaming about her. He never watched Brooke and Gabe together without conjuring up her beautiful face. She stayed with him every moment of every day, and he could sit home and think of her, or he could go to church where he belonged and submerse himself in worship.

Longing for the peace and renewal of worship, he decided against staying home. Besides, he'd have to see Kylie on Thursday evening for their shift on the help line anyway. What difference would a glimpse of her on Sunday make?

Famous last words. The instant he turned the Jeep into the parking lot at the church, he saw Kylie. Standing next to an unfamiliar car, she appeared to be in a conversation with the driver, that Janey woman from the diner and the Independence Day picnic. The discussion looked much too intense for picking colors and background music. It was none of his business, so he did his best to ignore it as he parked and made his way inside.

He barely set foot in the building before Reverend West had him by the hand. "Zach, you'll be staying for the Volunteer Appreciation Luncheon today, won't you? I want to introduce our newest additions to the rest of the volunteer team. The ladies have put together quite a spread. I understand your cousin Arabella has baked a special cake." He winked. "In fact, I think she told me it was your favorite."

Zach knew a trap when he walked into one. Since his return to town, he hadn't spent as much time with Arabella and her girls as he'd have liked, but he'd been around her place enough to know that she made a killer German chocolate cake. He'd done his best to make himself sick on the same just this past week. His mouth watered now at the very thought of it. Arabella eked a living, such as it was, out of her baking, and she'd been tickled by his enthusiasm. Obviously, she'd made an effort to please him with today's dessert selection.

Knowing that he'd offend the pastor and his cousin if he skipped out on the luncheon, Zach smiled and said, "I'll stay."

"Good man!" the reverend praised, slapping Zach on the back.

Zach joined his sister and Gabe for the worship service. Kylie, as usual, sat with her family. Zach noticed that her friend Janey had not come inside, but he saw his Aunt Lisette slip in at the last moment and waved. Quelling his curiosity about Janey, he focused on worship, and the time flew by. Before he knew it, everyone was making for the doors at the back of the sanctuary. A good number of the congregation headed toward the Fellowship Hall in the Annex, including Brooke and Gabe and the three elder Joneses.

Tables with pristine white cloths and folding chairs had been set up, and a lengthy buffet was quickly filled up with dishes of fried chicken, creamed potatoes, green beans, corn and a number of salads and casseroles. Zach glanced at the dessert table, where Arabella busily cut uniform pieces of her German chocolate sheet cake. Wedges of cherry pie and blocks of green Jell-O had already been dished up. Waving a chocolate-and-coconut-smeared knife at him, Arabella grinned. Zach blew her kisses from his spot in the buffet line, making her laugh.

"Uh-huh, I see what's going on here," Gabe teased Zach. "It's dessert nepotism, pure and simple. I voted for cheesecake. Have you ever eaten Arabella's cheesecake? I'm telling you, the groom's cake at our wedding better be Arabella's cheesecake."

"Is that legal?" Zach quipped. "I think the wedding police may have something to say about that."

"Oh, I guess you're the wedding police now, too, huh?"

Brooke elbowed her fiancé, saying, "Uh, that would be *me*. Or Kylie." She thumped Zach in the chest. "She's an excellent wedding planner, you know."

"I know," Zach grumbled. "She apprenticed in Denver." And she meant to go back there as soon as possible.

The pastor called for attention and gave thanks for the food, then those lined up on either side of the buffet began filling their plates. It didn't take long for Zach's party to get their turn.

As soon as they picked a table to bear their overloaded plates, Brooke went to get A.J. from the church nursery while Gabe hunted up a booster chair for the boy. Zach sat down to "guard the goodies," as Gabe jokingly put it. He was sipping from a glass of sadly weak iced tea when Darlene and Macy showed up with their own plates.

"Are these seats taken?"

"No, they're not," Zach replied, rising to pull out chairs for them. "Sit right down."

Macy, he noticed with a smile, took the chair next to his. Darlene got her daughter settled, then took her own seat. As Zach assisted her with her chair, she tilted her head back to look up at him.

"Thanks. I'm really glad for a chance to talk to you today."

"Why's that?" Zach asked as he resumed his own seat.

Mother and daughter traded looks. "Well," Darlene began, "we were talking to the pastor the other day, and he mentioned that in larger cities they have organizations that provide male companionship for fatherless children."

"You mean like Big Brothers?"

"Yes. Exactly."

"So," Macy said nervously, picking up the narrative, "we

were wondering, if it wasn't too much trouble, if you might
be my 'big brother' like Gabe is. If you want to, I mean…"

Zach relaxed back in his chair and tapped his chin with a
forefinger. "Hmm," he said, pretending ambivalence, "I already have two little sisters." Macy dropped her gaze to her
plate, biting her lip. Zach leaned forward and softly added,
"I'd love to have three."

She launched out of her chair with a squeal and threw her
arms around his neck. *I had three little sisters once,* Zach
thought, swallowing a lump in his throat. *It would be good
to have three sisters again, even if one of them was only
pretend.* Caught up in the moment, he gave her a hug. She
abruptly pulled away, declaring, "I'm gonna go tell Lily!"

She rushed off before her mother could admonish her.
Darlene gave Zach an exasperated look and pushed back her
chair. "If I don't go get her, she'll forget all about her lunch."
Chuckling, he got to his feet again as she rose. "Thank you
so much," Darlene paused to say. "You don't know what this
means to us."

"My pleasure," Zach told her, and she moved away. It was
true. Macy had stolen his heart in ways he had not expected.

"Well done," said a familiar voice at his elbow. Steeling
himself, Zach turned to face Kylie, who stood beside him
with a plate of food in one hand and a plastic tumbler of iced
tea in the other.

She looked amazing in a muted green dress that perfectly
matched her eyes. The armholes of the sleeveless, tailored
knit sheath had been cut wide and high, calling attention to
the little stand-up collar that lovingly circled her long, grace-
ful neck. With her long, crinkly hair down and loose, just the
sides caught together at the back of her head, pink lipstick
and narrow gold hoops dangling from her tiny earlobes, she
appeared both otherworldly and powerfully feminine. Just
looking at her made him ache with longing.

"You've taken quite an interest in that little girl," Kylie said softly.

"She's a sweet kid," Zach said, trying—and failing—to look away.

"A sweet kid in need of more positive male influences in her life. Gabe's great with her, but he's also got his hands full with A.J."

"Yeah, I guess that's why they asked me to be like a big brother to her."

Kylie smiled. "I think they chose well."

Pleased and a little embarrassed by that, Zach looked away. "I, uh, just hope I'm not too busy to give her the attention she needs."

"Another busy week then?" Kylie asked. "I thought as much. Haven't seen you around. Just barely caught a glimpse of you on Thursday before you were called away."

Zach cleared his throat. "Sorry to have left you alone with that."

"Oh, it wasn't anything I couldn't handle," she said. "But it was lonely." She tilted her head, adding, "I've missed you."

He thought he'd melt right where he stood. She had missed him. He'd intentionally kept away, and she had not only noticed, she had actually missed him. *Who am I kidding?* he thought. His intention to keep his distance had less to do with Vincent than with his own fear of getting his heart broken. How stupid could he be? What difference did it make, really, if he got shot down? He had zero chance if he didn't *try*. The time had come to stop behaving like a thirteen-year-old kid and act his age. He had finally met a woman who twisted his guts into knots then untied them again just by saying that she'd missed him. He had an opportunity here; he'd be an idiot not to take it.

He quickly began shifting Brooke's plate to the far side of Gabe's. At the same time he said, "Want a seat?"

She favored him with a bright smile. "Don't mind if I do."

He jumped to pull out and hold her chair. Before he could sit down beside her, Darlene and Macy returned to the table. Gabe showed up in time to get Brooke's chair and settle A.J. before the pastor claimed everyone's attention to thank all the volunteers who kept the ministries of the church going. He then asked all of the new volunteers who had come on board since the last luncheon to rise and introduce themselves. Kylie and Zach rose together. He didn't think a thing about it until Brooke and Gabe did the same. Of course, everyone knew that Brooke and Gabe were a couple. Maybe he and Kylie would be, too.

That's what Zach had in mind when Gene and Lynette came by the table a bit later. "We're ready to head out, hon," Lynette said to Kylie.

Before Kylie could even push back her chair, Zach said, "Don't worry about her. I'll run her home later. After we've had our dessert."

To his immense satisfaction, Kylie relaxed and smiled up at her parents. Gene grinned and guided his wife away. "Come on. Let's leave the youngsters to their sweets."

"Speaking of sweets," Zach said, getting up. "I'm eating two pieces of that cake."

Everyone laughed, but he meant what he said. In fact, he wound up gulping down two and a half pieces, since Kylie proclaimed herself unable to finish hers. The luncheon ended all too soon, but Zach didn't mind having Kylie all to himself on the drive out to her parents' place. She seemed content to ride in silence, but he did not mean to let another opportunity pass by him.

"I like your dress," he told her. "Almost as much as the first one I saw you in."

She laughed. "Thanks. I'd just as soon forget the first one, though."

"I never will," he told her. "I think you made the most beautiful bride I've ever seen."

The smile she gave him set his heart racing. "Thank you. I'm just glad I made a bride and not a *wife*. At least, in that case."

He couldn't have agreed more heartily. "That makes two of us. If you were married, I couldn't ask you out to dinner again."

"And if I were married," she replied, "I couldn't accept."

Zach had to grin. He hadn't even said *when* they might go to dinner, yet she'd already agreed. "How's Tuesday sound? Gabe and Brooke have invited me over. I'm sure they wouldn't mind including you."

"Good. I'll make sure when I go in to work tomorrow that I get Tuesday evening off."

"Okay." The Jeep shuddered as it passed over the cattle guard at the end of the drive at the Jones place. "I'll pick you up here around six then."

"I look forward to it," she said as he brought the vehicle to a stop. She opened her door, but then she paused. "Oh, and while I'm thinking of it, I never did thank you for helping Dad clean up the truck. Actually, I didn't realize all that you'd done until Dad told me."

He shrugged nonchalantly. "Glad I could help."

"You didn't have to," she told him. "It's certainly not in your job description, and I do appreciate it." Then she leaned over and pressed a lingering kiss to his cheek.

If his lungs hadn't suddenly stopped working and his brain hadn't frozen, he'd have turned his head and brought his lips to hers, but by the time he could function again, she'd slipped away. That kiss would have to hold him for another two days.

Somehow, he thought it would do, but that didn't mean he wouldn't be seeing her in the meantime.

From here on out, he had every intention of not just seeing Kylie but of courting her. And if Vincent didn't like it, that was his problem.

For the first time, Kylie understood that old saying about walking on air. Despite her misgivings and the threat to her cherished dreams, she could not contain her delight and excitement at the prospect of going on a date with Zach. Even as she feared falling in love with him, she felt absurdly happy and hopeful. Mariette noticed first, followed by their parents. Erin noticed, too, and drew some erroneous conclusions.

"Wow, this secret admirer of yours has certainly put a smile on your face." Unfortunately, she made that remark in the diner in front of one of Vincent's friends, and denying it did Kylie no good.

"Those flowers were somebody's idea of a joke, nothing more."

"Some joke," Erin quipped. "Wish someone would play that kind of joke on me."

"No, you don't," Kylie muttered, glancing at Vincent's buddy, whose ears might as well have been twitching. He'd leaned so far over the counter that his behind couldn't possibly have been touching his stool.

A few minutes later, Erin invited Kylie to join a group of her coworkers the next evening for a "movie night" after the diner closed. The staff of the Cowboy Café did this fairly regularly, and Kylie always brought the popcorn and others provided soft drinks and chocolate. Vincent had hated that she would go without him, but "staff only" was a hard and fast rule of these gatherings. Kylie had never considered ditching her friends and coworkers just to please him. This time, however, Kylie had no problem telling Erin that she had other plans.

Erin stared at her in shock for all of two minutes. "A joke, she calls it. Well, I guess those flowers have you laughing with somebody special."

"No, really," Kylie insisted. "He didn't send those flowers."

"Ah-ha!" Erin cried gleefully. "I knew there was someone! Spill, girlfriend. Who are you seeing?"

Kylie glanced at Vincent's friend, who appeared to be taking his jolly good time over his lunch plate, and snagged Erin by the sleeve of her Western-style shirt, hauling her to a far corner, where she whispered, "It's Zach, okay? But keep it to yourself, will you?" She went on to explain her suspicions concerning the flowers and the brooch delivered to the Feed & Supply.

"That's pretty sneaky, even for Vincent," Erin said, sounding a bit doubtful.

"There's no other explanation," Kylie insisted. "He's trying to make the men in this town believe I'm already seriously involved with someone so they'll keep their distance."

"He's obviously not succeeding," Erin pointed out with a waggle of her eyebrows. "Zach's apparently interested."

Kylie had to smile. "Maybe. Time will tell."

That afternoon, however, time did nothing but crawl. Despite working a busy double shift that day so she could take the time to go out the following night, Kylie felt antsy and impatient. She spent the evening deciding what to wear for her dinner date with Zach, settling on a pair of brown jeans and a matching tank top worn beneath a short, fitted, turquoise-blue jacket.

She had apparently chosen well because when Zach arrived to pick her up for their date, he looked her over with obvious appreciation, saying, "No wonder turquoise is your favorite color. It looks great on you. But then, what doesn't?"

Laughing, she thanked him. Her father turned from his television program then and invited Zach to sit down for a visit, but Zach politely refused.

"Gabe was heating the grill when I left. We wouldn't want to keep those T-bone steaks waiting too long."

"Think maybe I'll join you for dinner," Gene teased.

"Think again," Kylie and her mother chorused. Everyone laughed. As Kylie and Zach slipped out of the house, Lynette explained that Gene's cholesterol wouldn't allow him to eat "slabs" of steak.

Kylie noticed that Zach looked great in dark jeans and a pale blue shirt worn with the collar open and the sleeves rolled back. Moreover, he seemed to be in a great mood, laughing and teasing. When they got to his house, they didn't even go in, just walked across the backyard and through a gap in a hedge to Gabe's patio. He tended the grill while Brooke laid plates on a round, glass-topped table and A.J. stared, enchanted, at the twinkle of fireflies in the gloomiest corner of the yard nearest the creek.

Immediately after the adults greeted each other, Zach went to A.J. and, crouching down beside the boy, spoke to him softly about the tiny lights flashing in the dusky darkness. After a moment, A.J. wound a little arm around Zach's neck and leaned against him. The big, tough deputy sheriff really had a way with kids. He would, Kylie thought, make a great dad. As if to underscore that idea, Zach caught up the boy and rose, turning with him to face the group.

"Book, Book," the boy called, pointing over Zach's shoulder. "Is bugs!"

"I know," Brooke said, going to chuck A.J. under the chin. "Maybe after dinner Uncle Zach can take you down there to catch some."

"I'm a lightning bug chaser from way back," Zach said, patting the child on the head. He winked at Kylie.

Grinning, she impulsively challenged him. "I say I can catch more fireflies than you can."

"Well, we'll just have ourselves a *lightning bug* hunt right after dinner then." Pretending seriousness, they shook hands on it, then a grinning Zach turned to Gabe. "Anything I can do to help get that cow on the plate so I can put this beautiful braggart in her place?"

"You're doing it," Gabe told him, nodding at A.J.

Zach lifted A.J. over his head, declaring, "Finally, I've made 'designated player'! I knew all that slacking would pay off someday." Zooming like an airplane, he dipped and whirled. A.J. put out his arms and giggled with delight.

Kylie watched from the corner of her eye while she helped Brooke get the rest of the food on the table.

"He's always been good with kids," Brooke told her softly. "You should have seen him with our baby sister Lucy."

Kylie's head jerked around. Brooke had never mentioned Lucy to her before, certainly not in so easy a manner. "He's certainly good with Macy," she managed, "but I've never seen him like this."

"Happy, you mean?" Brooke adjusted the placement of the salad bowl. "You're at least partly responsible for that, you know."

"Me?"

"He's been so much more relaxed since you got him to open up about what happened in Miami."

"Oh, but I didn't do anything," Kylie protested, "except listen."

Brooke lifted an eyebrow. "I can name half a dozen people who would be willing to listen to anything Zach might have to say, myself included, but you're the one he could talk to."

Kylie didn't know what to say to that, but she couldn't help smiling. Could it be true? Did Zach find it easy to talk to her about the things that mattered most to him? If so, what did it mean? And why did the idea please her so much?

She had never felt this spurt of satisfaction and delight at pleasing Vincent. Shame filled her because she knew that she had never felt for Vincent what she should have. She'd wanted to marry him for all the wrong reasons, selfish reasons. God had shown her the error of her ways, and then He'd promptly brought Zach into her life. But what did that mean? Could God be so good as to bring her real love this time?

She didn't doubt that she could love Zach, but could he love her in return? She shocked herself by hoping so. Maybe the time had come for a new dream.

Chapter Ten

Kylie smiled all through dinner. Afterward, while she and Zach raced around with A.J., and somehow managed not to catch a single "li'tin' bug," Kylie laughed until her sides hurt. Finally, A.J. crawled into his daddy's lap, exhausted. Kylie collapsed into her chair, while Zach dragged his away from the table so he could sit down and stretch out his long legs. Within minutes, the boy fell asleep. Gabe held him for perhaps half an hour while the adults joked about this season's particularly swift and cagey fireflies. Eventually Zach confessed that he hated to put any live thing in a jar, especially something so beautiful. Kylie admitted that she, too, enjoyed chasing the tiny insects more than catching them.

"You know what we have here," Gabe teased. "A pair of frauds."

"Well, they're a pair anyway," Brooke put in.

Kylie couldn't resist glancing at Zach. He'd put his head back and closed his eyes, but his lips curled in a private smile. Kylie lowed down to hide her own. The thought of being paired with Zach filled her with joy. She knew intellectually that indulging these feelings was asking for trouble, but she couldn't regret these moments of sweet bliss. Where they would lead, though, only God knew.

When Brooke and Gabe rose a few minutes later to put A.J. to bed, Kylie and Zach kept their chairs. Neither said a word, each lost in their own thoughts. As the night gathered around them, Kylie became aware of a sense of peace. She watched Zach, who all but reclined in his chair, hands folded just above his belt, head back and eyes closed.

Earlier, Brooke had described him as happy, but Kylie now realized that went for her, too. She hadn't felt really happy in so long that she almost hadn't recognized the emotion. She said a quick, silent prayer of gratitude. When she glanced his way, she found Zach staring at her, almost as if he sensed that she had approached the Throne of Heaven in prayer. He put out his hand, and without hesitation, Kylie placed her own in it. Squeezing her fingers, he readjusted his position and closed his eyes again. Kylie smiled, utterly content.

Around ten, after an evening of lively if inconsequential conversation, Zach drove Kylie home. To her surprise, her father appeared in the front doorway even before Zach brought the vehicle to a stop. Calling out to them, he insisted that Zach come inside. Kylie rolled her eyes. He'd pulled that same trick with Vincent, but it had come weeks after they'd started dating. She couldn't say so, though, without embarrassing both herself and Zach. For his part, Zach just chuckled and shrugged.

"A few minutes won't hurt, I guess."

They went inside, but Kylie stayed on alert, ready to head off her father if he so much as hinted that Zach might have "intentions" toward her. Her mother, as usual, had turned in early, and Mariette chatted on the phone with one of the girls assigned to her dorm room at college. Thanks to social networking, the two were well on their way to becoming fast friends before they could even meet face to face. Gene shut off the television, invited Zach to sit on one of the denim-upholstered chairs that flanked the quilt-covered sofa and asked how their night had gone.

Zach entertained him with stories of A.J. and the great bug chase before asking, "So, no more vandalism issues?"

"Nope. Maybe he got it out of his system."

No one had to name the "he" in question.

"Maybe so," Zach said. Personally, Kylie doubted it, but she said nothing. "Well, I need to pound the pavement before starting work tomorrow," he went on, rising, "so I'd best turn in." Zach patted his taut belly. "Gotta run off that scrumptious T-bone."

"Rub it in, why don't you?" Gene groused good-naturedly.

Chuckling, Zach bade him good night.

"I'll walk you out," Kylie said, getting to her feet.

They stepped onto the porch. Light fixtures mounted on either side of the front door illuminated the immediate area.

"I had a great time tonight," she told him.

He grinned. "So lightning bugs are your thing, huh?"

"Fireflies," she countered, playfully thumping him on the chest.

Loosely looping his arms around her, he half propelled, half danced her into the shadows at the end of the porch, saying, "Fireflies, lightning bugs. Sounds like six of one and half a dozen of another to me."

Breathless with anticipation for what she sensed coming, Kylie managed to quip, "In other words, a rose is a rose by any other name?"

"More like, a lightning bug is a lightning bug by any other name."

Kylie laughed, but the gleam in his eye quickly sobered her. Smoothing his hands over her back, he gently pressed her closer and bent his head. Carefully, he fit his lips to hers, kissing her with patient, detailed thoroughness. When, at length, he broke the kiss, he simply held her, lightly pressing her head against his shoulder. She didn't recall wrapping her arms around his waist, but obviously at some point she had. It felt so good to be held by him, so safe. But that could be an illusion.

"Do you really think Vincent has moved on?" she asked quietly.

Zach didn't answer right away, but then he said, "No. That's not how my cousin operates." Lifting his hands, Zach tipped up her face, adding, "I don't want you worrying about him, though. It won't change anything. All it would do is make you miserable, and that would make everyone around you miserable. Including me."

Kylie smiled. "That's the last thing I want to do."

"Glad to hear it." He pressed his forehead to hers, the tips of their noses meeting, and closed his eyes. She let her eyelids drift down, and they stood in silent contentment for several seconds before he slowly pulled away. "I really ought to go."

"Thank you for a lovely evening," she told him.

"No, thank *you,*" he returned, backing away. "See you tomorrow?"

"Hope so."

"Tomorrow then. Sleep well."

"You, too," she whispered.

Bestowing a final smile, he turned away to stride quickly to his vehicle. He paused just before dropping down behind the steering wheel. Kylie waved, and he lifted a hand before starting up the Jeep and driving away. She watched until the red dots of his taillights disappeared into the distance before she went inside.

On his way to bed, her dad stopped to kiss her cheek and say teasingly, "The stars aren't just in the sky tonight." He tapped a forefinger between her eyes, patted her head and went on his way.

Perhaps she did have stars in her eyes, Kylie thought. What girl who had been out with Zach Clayton wouldn't?

It came as no surprise that Kylie dreamed of Zach that night, reliving every moment of their time together. She woke the next morning with the certainty that her feelings for Zach had grown by leaps and bounds. What ultimately came of them was up to God, but Kylie accepted that she had no choice but to see where they led her. She felt surprisingly upbeat about that. In fact, she felt downright giddy until she arrived at work the next morning to find Erin and Zach standing in front of the Cowboy Café, shaking their heads.

Kylie didn't have to ask why. It had been written on the diner windows in big, bold strokes with white shoe polish.

"I love you, beautiful Kylie! Be mine forever!"

"Oh, no!"

"Now, don't make more of it than it is," Zach said, coming to wrap his arms around her.

"Zach, you have to make him stop," she pleaded, horrified that her friend's property had been defaced because of her.

"We don't know that it's Vincent, Kylie."

"Of course it's Vincent!" She fumed. "He's behind it, at least."

"But we have no proof."

"Who else could have a reason for doing this?" she demanded, pulling away.

Sighing, Zach shook his head. In other words, he had no answers for her. Blinking back her tears, she stomped inside to fill a bucket with warm sudsy water and begin the task of cleaning the windows. Erin followed, murmuring reassurances.

"Hey, it's no big deal. Windows needed washing anyway."

"Sure," Kylie said mordantly, heading back outside. "If this keeps up you'll have the cleanest windows in town. Yippee."

As soon as she stepped through the door, Zach tried to reason with her.

"Kylie," he said in such a sensible tone of voice that she wanted to tag him with a wet sponge, "it's not like anyone's been hurt. I can't even plead property damage. I'm filing a report, of course, and I promise that I'll do my best to keep an eye on Vincent, but the most I can tell the sheriff is that folks have been irritated and caused a certain amount of inconvenience. There's just no basis for an arrest or a search warrant or the extra manpower needed to keep a constant watch on Vincent and his cohorts. Please try to understand."

"I understand," she told him through gritted teeth, scrubbing the soapy sponge over the window. "He's determined to make my life miserable. And he's succeeding."

"Don't let him," Zach counseled. "Don't give him that satisfaction." Erin appeared in the door with a rubber-edged scraper and a bucket of clean water. Zach plucked the scraper from her hand. "Here," he said, dipping it into the clean water, "I'll help you." But instead of applying the scraper to the window, he flicked his wrist, spraying water droplets over Kylie.

Gasping in surprise, she hopped back. While Erin snickered, Zach stood there with eyebrows cocked, a hopeful expression on his face. Kylie got it. She could cry or she could laugh, but although she knew Zach was right about not letting Vincent succeed at making her miserable, Kylie could not yet see any humor in the situation.

"If it was just me, I wouldn't care, but this—"

"Is pointless," Erin put in. "I mean, it's not working, right?" She pointed a finger at Zach. "He hasn't made you believe that Kylie's having some secret, clandestine…*thing* with some other guy, has he? You're not discouraged, are you?"

Zach held Kylie's gaze with his. "I'm not discouraged," he said softly.

Kylie felt a wan smile tug at her lips. Bending his arm, he leaned toward her and wiped a drop of water from the tip of her nose with his sleeve. Then he bent and picked up the bucket of soapy water. He winked and pulled back both arms as if preparing to throw the entire contents on her. Yelping, she jumped back, only to feel a bark of laughter escape as he turned at the last moment and sluiced the water over the windows of the diner, splattering himself liberally. Erin had managed to step back and push the door closed, but she yanked it open again an instant later. She glanced at Kylie, then they both stared at Zach.

"Okay," he muttered sheepishly, looking down at himself, "not my best idea."

Erin sputtered with laughter. Suddenly, they were all laughing so hard that Kylie could barely stand up straight. She forced herself to go back to work with the sponge, then watched, chuckling, while Zach scraped the window clean and Erin gathered up the buckets and sponge. Finished, Zach handed over the scraper, and Erin went inside to put everything away.

Zach dried his palms on his already damp thighs, tapped the end of Kylie's nose with the tip of one forefinger and announced that he could eat his weight in flapjacks; later, having attempted to do just that, he walked across the green to his office. Her equilibrium restored, Kylie went about her own business.

That afternoon, a box of chocolates arrived in the mail at the Feed & Supply. Mariette brought the package over to the diner. Determined to take Zach's advice to heart, Kylie mockingly read the card aloud. "Sweets for the sweetest of beauties."

Rolling her eyes, she passed around the goodies to the

diners, being certain to include anyone who hung out with Vincent.

A teddy bear wearing a red satin heart on its chest awaited her when she arrived at the diner the next morning. Kylie remarked loudly several times that day how sad it was that her "secret admirer" did not possess enough confidence to present himself to her in person. One of the guys from the mine remarked that the deputy sheriff must not be as bold as he appeared.

Over the snicker of his single companion, Erin refuted that with a wry glance in Kylie's direction. "That's not what I've heard."

The pink blooming in Kylie's cheeks only served to reinforce the insinuation. Lifting her chin, she beat back her embarrassment and added a secretive smile to the blush. Later, when Laura West, the pastor's wife, came in for lunch, Kylie made a production of donating the stuffed bear to the church nursery. By the time Zach came to walk her over to the church for their shift on the help line, Kylie felt somewhat in control of her life again.

That feeling intensified later when, taking a break to stretch her legs while Zach talked to an older man angry with his adult son, Kylie noticed Janey Guilder's car parked in front of the church. Kylie had spotted Janey cruising by the church on the Sunday morning just past. The two had talked for a while, and Janey had seemed troubled, but she'd refused to come inside or discuss what was bothering her. Sensing that much was wrong in the young woman's life, Kylie had impulsively offered a willing ear anytime.

Kylie opened the door and went outside. Sobbing, Janey looked much the worse for wear now. The collar on her mint-green cotton blouse had been torn, and her face showed red marks already darkening to bruises. Remembering a similar bruise at the base of Janey's throat, Kylie insisted that the weeping brunette come inside the building with her.

"Janey, tell me what's happened."

"I—I shouldn't have c-come here," the other woman said haltingly. "I just d-didn't know where else to go! My f-father said he'd k-kill him if he did this again!"

"Rob," Kylie surmised, guiding Janey down the hall toward the office where Zach manned the phones. "Rob hit you, didn't he?"

"H-he doesn't mean to do it. The d-drink makes him do it."

"So it's happened before," Kylie said, her suspicions confirmed. What were a few prank gifts and a little shoe polish compared to that? And to think she'd let those silly things shake her!

Zach saw them coming and managed to get off the phone in time to rise to his feet as Kylie steered Janey through the door of the room. Recognizing him, Janey balked, but Kylie urged her forward.

"Zach can help if you let him."

Janey shook her head. "I—I don't want Rob arrested. That would only make things worse. My dad works for his family."

Zach flashed Kylie a look as he came around the computer table to assess Janey's condition. That one glance telegraphed frustration, resignation and determination, but his manner toward Janey could not have been more patient or supportive.

"I'm no doctor," he said after quietly asking several questions to determine the extent of her injuries. "For the record, I strongly urge you to seek medical assistance. But from what I can tell, bruising seems to be the extent of the physical damage. This time."

Kylie pulled a chair around for Janey to sit on then went to lean against the edge of the computer table beside Zach.

"I don't need a doctor," Janey whispered.

"Maybe, maybe not," Zach said, "but I still urge you to see one, if only to document your condition."

Janey looked away. Zach leaned forward, his hands braced on his thighs.

"This time was worse than the last one, wasn't it?" he probed carefully. Janey's surprised gaze zipped back to him. "And the time between episodes is getting shorter and shorter. Right?"

"It's the drinking," Janey insisted. "He only gets rough when he's drinking."

"Sure, I understand," Zach said. "Every abuser has an excuse, and booze is often it, but he doesn't quit drinking, does he? Oh, he apologizes and pleads for more chances and swears that he loves you, but when it comes to a choice between your welfare and his alcohol, he always chooses the alcohol." He sighed heavily. "He'll swear that he's not an alcoholic and admit that the booze makes him hurt you, but he won't give it up. Instead, he tells you that it's your fault because you know how the drinking affects him and insist on irritating him to the point that he has to smack you around. That about right?"

Janey looked haunted. "Kind of."

"The rest of the time he's a peach," Zach went on. "A little gruff, a bit demanding, somewhat critical, but that's your fault, too. You just don't know how to act around him."

Janey locked her gaze on her hands. "I do t-try."

"Yeah, but the requirements keep changing, don't they? What worked for you one time doesn't work the next."

Tears began to drip from Janey's eyes and splash on her hands. "I don't know what to do anymore."

"Get out before he seriously injures or even kills you," Zach said starkly. Leaning forward, he grasped the arms of her chair and spoke urgently. "Why can't he read you and discern your needs at any given moment?"

"But that's unreasonable," she muttered. "No one can do that."

"Isn't that what he expects of you, though?"

Janey bit her lip. "It seems like it is."

"Okay. Ask yourself this. If the booze makes him do things that he doesn't want to do, then why doesn't he give it up? Is it because he can't or because he just doesn't want to?"

"I d-don't know!" she sobbed.

"Yes, you do," Zach said quietly. "But he's convinced you that no other man could ever want you, and like the rest of us, you fear being alone, so you take what he dishes out even though you can see that it's getting worse and becoming the norm in your relationship." Zach went down on his haunches before her, saying softly, "Weak men abuse women because it makes them feel strong. He does these things to you because he secretly *likes* to do them, only the rush wanes over time, and he has to escalate the violence to keep getting the same confidence boost. He needs that feeling, and when his conscience kicks him or the world shows its disapproval, he'll blame you. That allows him to beat you again. Don't stay until he hits you hard enough to snap your neck or chokes the life out of you."

"You have to get away from him, Janey," Kylie put in, laying a hand on the other woman's shoulder.

"Let me pick him up," Zach urged.

"No! I told you. That will just make everything worse."

"I can't promise it won't happen even without your cooperation," Zach told her. "I have to write a report, and if similar incidents have been filed in the past, the county sheriff may direct me to pick him up, but it would be easier if you'd file charges."

"I can't."

"Even if he doesn't get jail time, he could be forced into counseling."

"I don't care," Janey declared, straightening her spine. "Let the next woman worry about it."

Kylie traded looks with Zach. "Then you'll at least break your engagement?"

"I already have," Janey revealed, lifting her left hand to show her bare finger. "I threw the ring at him as I ran out of his house."

"You've done it before, though, haven't you?" Zach guessed.

Wide-eyed, Janey nodded. "How did you know?"

"Because I've seen this pattern play out a hundred times before," Zach told her, pushing up to his full height again.

"You have to mean it this time, Janey," Kylie pleaded. "Please. I don't want to see you hurt even worse."

Janey sighed and nodded.

"God has someone else picked out for you," Zach assured her, "someone who will treat you with the respect and care you deserve. The right man will put you before everything else in his life except God, and he'll encourage you to do the same thing for him. If it hurts you, he won't do it. In fact, he'll bend over backward to lift you up."

"Wow," Janey said in an awed voice.

"Yes. Wow," Kylie echoed softly, gazing at Zach. She knew she had stars in her eyes again.

"But why would God pick out a guy for me?" Janey asked.

"Because He loves you and wants you to be happy," Zach told her. "He loves you so much that He made His own Son a sacrifice for your sins. You see, we all sin, even the very best of us, and sin creates a chasm between us and God. Jesus is our bridge. He closes the gap and allows us to draw near to Him in prayer."

"You can do that?" Janey asked, glancing from one to the other of them.

"We can do it right now if you want," Zach said, glancing

at Kylie for confirmation. She nodded her head. He reached for her hand then held out his other one to Janey. Kylie followed suit. Hesitantly, Janey placed her hands in theirs. Zach bowed his head, leaning his shoulder against Kylie's, and began to pray aloud. "Heavenly Father, thank You for bringing Janey here tonight. Please give her strength and wisdom to do the best thing for herself. Help her to know and accept Your love for her so that she can know and accept the love of another. Whoever the man is You've picked out for her, we ask You to bless him and hold him apart for her. Bring them together when the time is right. Meanwhile, Lord, we ask You to give her peace. We ask, too, that You show Rob how to find true happiness in his own life. We know that our happiness rests in You and living a life pleasing to You…"

When he came to the end of his prayer, he squeezed Kylie's hand. Moved to speak, she did so, thanking God for her new friend and asking Him to keep Janey safe. Janey's grip tightened and she sniffled when Kylie said that. After ending her prayer in the name of Christ, Kylie moved forward to hug Janey, who then thanked both Kylie and Zach. Kylie walked Janey out of the building. Along the way, she invited Janey to church.

Nodding, Janey tilted her head, sniffed and said, "I'm afraid you've lost a client, though."

"I don't care," Kylie told her. "All that matters is that you stay safe and stop letting yourself be bullied. You deserve better."

"I was looking forward to working with you."

"We can still spend time together," Kylie told her. "In fact, let's have lunch soon."

For the first time since her arrival, Janey smiled. "I'd like that."

They hugged again before parting.

Kylie returned to find Zach, waiting pensively. "Think she'll stick to her guns this time?" he asked, coming forward.

"I hope so."

"Me, too. I'd feel better if she'd press charges, though." He crossed his arms. "Then again, I'd feel better if I could toss Vincent into a cell, and we know that's not happening. Not yet, anyway. By the way, I meant what I said about keeping an eye on things where he's concerned."

"I know you'll do everything you can."

Zach sighed and clapped a hand to the back of his neck. "It's maddening. I've got two guys who deserve to be jailed, and I can't touch either one."

"It is frustrating," Kylie agreed, "but I guess we just have to trust that there are reasons why things have been allowed to go this way."

"That's true. God surely has His reasons, and we can trust that they are ultimately for our benefit. We just have to be patient."

Patience, Kylie mused. A lack of patience had led her to look for a seemingly easy solution to her family's financial issues. Impatience and selfishness had led her astray. She felt very foolish. What might she have missed if she hadn't caught Vincent with another woman on their wedding day? Too much, she realized, looking at Zach. Maybe everything that God had planned for her.

Chapter Eleven

Yawning, Zach stretched his arms. He'd been sitting here for hours in his dark office, keeping a bleary eye on the Cowboy Café across the green. For several nights now, he'd been cruising by the diner and Feed & Supply every few hours in hopes of catching Vincent or one of his minions in the act of dropping off a package for Kylie or defacing property. He'd seen nothing suspicious, but at least he'd made himself visible enough that the harassment appeared to have halted.

Zach had begun to wonder, however, if he'd made himself *too* visible. He couldn't keep up these patrols indefinitely, after all. He had to sleep sometime, so he'd decided to take a more subtle approach. By leaving the Jeep at home and walking over to the office to sit in the dark with a pair of binoculars, he'd been able to keep watch over the diner and the approach to the Feed & Supply without showing himself.

With the hour approaching three o'clock in the morning, though, he'd begun to rethink this new approach. If something didn't happen soon, all he'd have to show for his Friday night would be boredom and weariness. Ah, well, at least Kylie wouldn't have any troubling gifts waiting for her when she arrived for the morning shift. He mused—not for the first time—that she worked too much and wished that he could find some way to lighten the family's financial burden so she could take off more time.

It was none of his business, of course.

But maybe the time had come to make it his business.

However, he had to ask himself if Kylie was ready for that. Was *he* ready for it? He certainly had not known her very long, and yet he felt as if he'd always known her somehow. He thought of her constantly, and being with her felt like the most exciting and the most natural thing in the world.

He didn't know what to do about her, so he did what he'd been doing increasingly since he'd come back home: he talked it over with God. Even as his gaze tracked back and forth between Railroad Street and Hawk Street, he prayed, a habit he'd developed on other lonely stakeouts.

We both know I care about her. In fact, I can't remember ever caring more for a woman. But is this the woman and the time You have planned for me? She seems to care, even after knowing the worst about me. But how much? And for how long? A little while ago, I was convinced that I ought to put distance between us, but we saw how well that worked out. Now what? I know what I want to do, but is it the right step?

His cell phone rang. At 3:00 a.m. That couldn't be good.

Reaching into his pocket, he rolled his eyes toward the ceiling, muttering, "Hope that's You with an answer, Lord."

Zach put the little phone to his ear. "Zach Clayton here."

Gene Jones' trembling voice replied. "We've got a fire at our place! Somebody set a fire!"

The binoculars clattered to the floor as Zach leapt to his feet. "On my way! Get everybody out of the house."

"Doing it now."

Zach tore out of the office and jumped into the county car, barking, "Call the fire brigade."

"Will do."

Zach shut off the phone and started the car. Lights flashing and siren wailing, he flew through town and barreled down Waxwing Road, the old sedan bouncing over the ruts. He could see a bright glow against the horizon. Two minutes later, dust and gravel spewed from beneath the rear tires as Zach yanked the wheel to make the turn into the driveway at the Jones place. Up this close, he could see that the blaze seemed to be coming from the back of the house.

Lynette stood in the front yard wrapped in a yellow terrycloth bathrobe, her feet bare and her gray-streaked hair mussed. The anxiety on her face matched Zach's. Throwing an arm to the side, she pointed left.

"Back there. Right outside Kylie's bedroom window."

Zach took off running. All he heard was "Kylie's bedroom," and that spurred him toward panic. *God, no!* he pleaded, running through the deep-black night shadows at the end of the house, the crackle and heat of the fire growing with every step. *Not Kylie. I beg You!* He almost tripped over something on the ground, realizing only as he left it behind that it had to be a water hose. *Please, not her!*

Rounding the corner, he saw a blaze as tall as the house but about ten feet away from it. He realized at once that a tree had been set afire, but that paled in comparison to the familiar silhouette limned by the flames. The cloud of Kylie's long hair seemed ablaze, but the way she calmly aimed a spray of water at the house, wetting down the logs so that the fire could not spread, belied that illusion. Her father, meanwhile, aimed another hose at the burning tree while Mariette stood with a filled bucket in hand, ready to douse any sparks that fell to the grass not already soaked.

Without anything in his head except pure relief, Zach ran straight to Kylie and threw his arms around her.

"Thank God! When your mother said it was your bedroom, I—I thought… I feared…" He was aware of the hose hitting the ground and water spraying his pant legs, but nothing mattered except knowing Kylie was safe and holding her close.

"It's okay," she said, rubbing a hand over his back. "It's just the bigtooth maple. They set fire to the tree outside my bedroom window. That's what Mom meant."

His racing pulse slowing somewhat, Zach made himself loosen his hold. A little. "You saw them?"

"No." Pulling away a bit, she shook her head, her hands flattening against his chest. "I woke to a loud *whoosh* and saw the light. When I looked out the window, the flames were already head high. I yelled, 'Fire!' and ran for the water hose. When Dad came out, he told me he'd called you."

Zach nodded, his brain beginning to function fully again. He saw that she wore baggy pajama bottoms and soggy sheepskin house shoes beneath a ragged aqua-blue chenille robe. In his eyes, she had never looked more beautiful.

"A *whoosh*," he echoed, bludgeoning his thoughts onto a useful path. "That means an accelerant was used."

"That's what we figured," Gene said, stomping up in unlaced work boots.

He'd donned his overalls without a shirt. Mariette, Zach saw, had taken over the other water hose. The flames had decreased in size, but Gene picked up the hose that Kylie had dropped and aimed it at the now skeletal tree.

"Did you call the fire brigade?" Zach asked, facing the man. He kept an arm around Kylie despite some embarrassment at embracing the man's daughter in front of him.

Gene shook his head. "Nah. Once I realized what was burning, I figured we could handle it without calling out the volunteers. Besides, Vincent and a bunch of his friends are on the volunteer list, and I didn't want them out here gawking and making jokes."

Zach nodded, feeling as if he'd run for miles. "Okay. I'd

like you to come by the office tomorrow and sign a report, if you will."

"No problem. Sorry I got you out at this time of the morning."

Zach shook his head, too relieved to be upset. "I was awake anyway, and I'm off tomorrow, so I can sleep half the day, if I need to." He reached for the hose, adding, "Now, let's get this put out."

Gene yielded the hose and clomped off to take over for Mariette. "Go tell your mother that we've got it under control."

She left the bucket on the ground and went into the house through a back door, returning a few minutes later with mugs of something hot. "It's apple cider," she told her father. "Mama says she's making breakfast, but you can't have coffee because she wants you to lay down again for a little while." She turned to Zach, who still had one arm around her sister. "And that goes for you, too." Grinning broadly, she thrust a mug at him before passing the last one to Kylie and going back into the house.

He'd removed his arm from Kylie's shoulders in order to grasp the mug, but he noticed that she didn't move away. Instead, she stood cradling her steaming mug in her hands with her shoulder touching his. Gulping down the fragrant cider, Zach had to work at not tossing aside the mug and wrapping his arm around her waist.

Eventually, Kylie went inside to change her clothes. Zach kept glancing at the back door until she returned, wearing jeans, sneakers and a dark gold sweatshirt, to take a seat on the edge of the back stoop. She answered Zach's questions as he aimed water at the tree.

No, she hadn't spoken to Vincent lately. He'd come into the diner on Friday, but another of the waitresses had seen to him. He'd sent over a message that he wanted to talk to her, but she'd said she was too busy, and eventually he'd left. She didn't know what sort of mood he'd been in when he'd gone out the door because she had studiously ignored him. He had left a message on her cell phone at some point, but she had deleted it without listening to it. Zach filed away the information for consideration later.

The hour approached 5:00 a.m. when he and Gene agreed that the tall, pointy stump of the tree harbored no glowing spark and put away the hoses. Kylie made sure that they both removed their boots, then she took a towel to Zach's and carried them through the house to the front door. He forced himself into a chair at the plank table in the kitchen to keep from following her despite the impulse not to let her out of his sight. If anything had happened to her... Shuddering at the thought, he felt a pat on his shoulder and looked around to find Lynette smiling down at him.

"Will you say a blessing for us, Zach?"

"Oh, um." He glanced over the table, shocked to find it weighted with the heartiest of breakfasts. "Sure. Lots to be thankful for, I see."

Gene chuckled. "Lynette cooks in a crisis."

"And rarely at any other time," Mariette added drolly, dropping into a chair across the table from Zach.

Kylie came and sat in the chair beside Zach, folding her hands and bowing her head. Zach couldn't stop himself from reaching out to cover her hands with his. She turned a palm against his and reached for her mother's hand with the other. Soon, they sat linked around the table, Gene's thick, heavy hand gripping Zach's on the other side.

Zach bowed his head and began to speak, words of relief and gratitude pouring out of him. By the time he finished, Gene's grip had intensified to the point where Zach began to think about bones cracking. Instead, his heart cracked open and love poured out for his God, this family and especially the woman whose small hand he held in his own.

"I didn't do nothing," Vincent sneered, "and you can't prove I did."

Unshaven, his hair spiking in every direction, he sprawled on the sofa in the living room of his small, dingy house, looking much the worse for wear. Of course, that might be because Zach had pounded on his door shortly after 6:00 a.m. He smirked at Zach over the chipped rim of a mug of coffee.

"Just answer the question," Zach instructed, standing over Vincent with his hands braced at his waist. "Where were you last night?"

"At a friend's place."

"Which friend?"

Vincent lifted his chin. "Rob Crenshaw. We had us a little drinking party, seeing as how we both had our women lured away."

"Lured away?" Zach scoffed. "Is that what you call getting caught cheating?"

"That meant nothing!" Vincent snapped, lurching forward to brace his elbows on his knees. "I'd have talked Kylie around if you hadn't got in between us."

"You obviously don't know Kylie as well as you think you do."

Vincent narrowed his eyes. "I suppose you think you know her better."

"I do. I also know that you can't win her back by harassing her."

Vincent left his cup on the scarred coffee table and leaned back again, grinning slyly. "Now, that's a contradiction in terms, don't you think? You can't have it both ways, law dog. Either I'm trying to get her back or I'm harassing her. Which is it?"

"We both know you seek to destroy what you can't have," Zach said.

Vincent's face clouded. "It's time for you to leave. I've answered your questions, and now I'm going back to bed."

Bed sounded good to Zach, too, but he had one more question. "What time did you get home this morning?"

"About five. I fell asleep on Rob's couch around two. His snoring woke me up a few hours later, so I came on home to get some real rest. Then you come pounding on my door to ask your questions without even telling me why."

"You know why," Zach said, unsurprised that Vincent had an alibi for the time that the fire had been set. He wondered which of his hangers-on Vincent had gotten to do his dirty work this time. "You should know, too, that I'm building a case against you, brick by brick." Vincent made a rude sound, which Zach ignored. "You crossed a boundary tonight, Vincent. What you did—or had done—was stupid and risky. Only by the grace of God was no real harm done, but your time's coming if you don't change your ways."

"The law can't touch me," Vincent said confidently.

"You don't think so?" Zach rested one hand meaningfully on the butt of his gun holster and leaned forward to loom over the smug man, the other hand braced on the back of the sofa. "One little misstep, that's all it'll take for this law dog to catch up to you. I'm telling you now that if Kylie so much as stubs her toe because of one of your stupid stunts, I'm coming after you, and the same goes for my sisters and cousins and their families, too." The cocky facade began to slip. Vincent drew back as Zach leaned closer still, adding, "This isn't the badge talking now, cuz. This is the Zach that used to beat you bloody for bullying my sisters in school. A bruise, a scrape, I don't care how seemingly minor. If one of them gets hurt, you get hurt, and that includes Kylie."

The bravado had faded completely now, replaced by

resentment. As Zach straightened, Vincent snarled, "Real Christian of you to threaten me."

"You think Christianity equates to cowardice, Vincent?" Zach asked mildly. "You think God would tell me *not* to protect others from bullies like you? If that's what you think, you need to seriously study the Bible."

An odd look flashed over Vincent's face. It seemed equal parts hunger, fear and vulnerability. That brief glance of common humanity in his old nemesis woke an unexpected empathy within Zach. He felt the sudden desire to reach out to the other man.

"Any time you want to explore the Bible, you call me. I'll be glad to help you. Believe it or not, Vincent, I don't want to be at loggerheads with you and yours." He sighed. "But I won't stand by while you harm or intimidate others. We can be friends or we can be enemies. It's entirely up to you. Think about that."

Sullen and silent, Vincent looked away, leaving Zach to wonder if he had imagined that instant of ambivalent yearning. Hoping that it had been real, he turned and walked out.

When he at last crawled into bed a few minutes later, he prayed that something he had said would have an impact on Vincent. The time had come for the Claytons—*all* the Claytons—to really be family again. He knew that God would not make the choice for Vincent and his side, but he prayed that hearts would be softened and minds opened, which reminded him of Cade. Maybe, Zach conceded, the kid was more on the ball than he had given him credit for. With that in mind, Zach prayed that he wouldn't have to get physical with Vincent—not because he doubted or feared his ability to come out on top of any altercation with his old nemesis, but because he earnestly desired peace between the branches of his family.

Kylie's well-being now took precedence over every other

consideration, however. That had to come first, even at the price of peace. Quite simply, she had become the most important person in Zach's life. She had become his personal responsibility, his to protect, and he suspected that it would always be so, no matter what the future held.

The ringing of his cell phone woke Zach mid-afternoon. He groaned, rolled over and found the instrument of torture on the bedside table. Making the connection, he sat up and cleared his throat.

"Zach Clayton."

The call was from his buddy in Florida, the state cop he'd asked to track down Lucas. The news troubled Zach, but at least he now knew *something*. Lucas had been staying in cheap motels around the Everglades but apparently never for more than one night at a time and always alone. Clearly, his cousin was on the run from someone, but who? And how could the family help him if they couldn't contact him? Did Lucas even know about the will?

Zach needed someone who could predict where Lucas would turn up next, instead of merely tracking where he'd been, but without proof of a threat or crime the state police couldn't go further. His buddy recommended an experienced private investigator and mentioned a name quite familiar to Zach, but he couldn't make this decision alone. He'd have to bring the girls in on this.

"Thanks, man. I appreciate all you've done, and I owe you for it."

"Hey," said his friend, "maybe I'll bring the wife to Colorado for a little snow skiing in the winter."

"Come on up," Zach said thoughtlessly. "We'll make it a foursome."

"Oh, yeah? You've got a better half now?"

Zach blinked, realizing that he'd automatically assigned

that role to Kylie. "Uh, not exactly. Let's just say I'm working on it."

"Now I've definitely got to get up to Colorado."

Laughing, Zach said, "The invitation stands." Then he got off the phone and forced his mind onto a pathway that did not, for once, lead directly to Kylie Jeanne Jones.

Ideally, Zach would have loaded up and headed back to Florida to search for Lucas himself. He had all the contacts and knowledge necessary to get the job done, but he also had a real job here. That and the possibility of violating the stipulations of his grandfather's will made it impossible for him to take on the task. Frustrated, he realized that he needed to speak to his sisters and cousins as soon as possible about hiring that private investigator.

Hauling himself out of bed, he headed for the shower. Half an hour later, he and Brooke walked up the pathway of Grandpa George's elegant old house on Railroad Street, just a block off the town green, where Arabella lived with her daughters and Jasmine. Together he and Brooke stepped up onto the deep, wraparound porch with its white wicker furniture and red flowering geraniums. Knowing that Arabella would likely be busy with her baking and the triplets, the cousins knocked, then let themselves in, the leaded glass front door being unlocked.

"Arabella?" Brooke called from the entry hall. A voice from the front parlor answered them.

"Brooke? Come join us."

Brooke walked into the living room. Zach tucked his sunshades into his shirt pocket and hung his hat on the coat tree before following her into the large, sprawling space. Despite a mixture of modern and antique furnishings, the room possessed a more formal aura than the smaller den where Arabella and the girls gathered to relax and watch television in the evening.

With her legs folded and bare feet tucked beneath her, Jasmine sat in the center of the long sofa that gave the room its focal point. Kylie sat beside her in her usual work attire, a laptop perched atop her knees. She flashed Zach a welcoming smile. Despite his delight at seeing her, he shifted his weight uneasily, sure he knew why she was here.

"Come look at the dresses," Jasmine said, eagerly waving them over.

Zach went to stand next to Brooke behind the sofa and peer over Kylie's shoulder. Wedding gowns, as feared. Zach said nothing, but he couldn't prevent a frown from dragging down the corners of his lips.

"I really like this one," Jasmine said, pecking the computer screen with a fingertip. "Isn't that gorgeous for a winter wedding?"

"It's pretty pricey, of course," Kylie cautioned, "so instead we could do something like…this." She clicked on a different tab. A screen came up showing a similar style of dress devoid of the costly embellishments. "It's a heavy knit, so we don't have to worry about alterations. Add our own trim, and we come up with the same look at a fraction of the cost. Actually, this style would be easy and inexpensive to make from scratch, too."

"Isn't that cool?" Jasmine gushed. "Kylie's got lots of great ideas like that. Show them the candles."

Kylie manipulated the view until a photo came up. She described how she would use sprigs of holly or mistletoe and natural greenery harvested from local landowners to create an inexpensive Christmas-themed décor purchasing only simple white candles and ribbon. While Brooke murmured appropriate remarks, Zach gritted his teeth.

A slight sound had Zach looking toward the doorway. Arabella leaned a shoulder against the casing, her wavy, golden-brown hair held back by a clip at the nape of her neck. Arms folded, she wore a loose, gauzy white blouse, gathered at the shoulders and belted at the waist with a length of braided cord, over comfy jeans and sandals. Running after her four-year-old triplets and worrying about Jasmine had kept the young single mother slender despite her occupation as a baker of excellent goodies.

Zach hated to think that she could lose her business along with this house if they failed to meet the requirements of their grandfather's will. Arabella had lived here with the old man after her divorce, and she'd cooked, cleaned and nursed him without a word of complaint to anyone. Grandpa George had repaid her by putting her home in jeopardy and used that to force his grandchildren to dance to his tune. Zach resented that on Arabella's behalf, yet, he couldn't deny that both he and Brooke had benefited from returning to Colorado.

Just how much remained to be seen.

Oh, no one could doubt that Brooke had found love, home and happiness here, but every time Zach thought he might have found the same, something cropped up to call that assumption into question, like a wedding that no one except the couple involved—and, apparently, Kylie—thought should take place.

What did that say about Kylie's judgment? And his?

Chapter Twelve

Arabella's golden eyes met Zach's across the large, formal parlor. He read and shared the disapproval and concern there, but she said nothing as Kylie expounded enthusiastically on her ideas for the wedding that Jasmine and Cade were planning.

When Kylie at last wound down, Arabella spoke. "Good to see you guys. Why don't you come back to the kitchen for a sample?"

"I thought you'd never ask," Zach quipped. He laid a hand on Kylie's shoulder, saying, "You could join us."

She tilted her head back, offering him a regretful smile. Then she glanced at Jasmine and her expression turned wary. When she looked back to Zach, her eyes seem to plead for his tolerance. "I, um, have a few more ideas to discuss with Jasmine."

He nodded and reluctantly left her there, Brooke following with a hand laid lightly against his back, as if to say that she understood his misgivings. They followed Arabella through the center of the house to the roomy, old-fashioned kitchen with its many windows and long butcher-block table. Despite the stark white cabinets, Arabella had given it a colorful feel with touches of green, yellow and red.

"Where are the girls?" Zach asked, pulling out a chair for his sister and another for Arabella.

"Taking naps, I hope," Arabella said, waving him down into his own chair. "Sit. I'll be there in a minute." She began filling a serving plate with goodies from various tins, pans and jars. As she worked, she spoke. "I don't know what to do about Jasmine. This wedding she's planning feels more real every day."

"What can you do?" Brooke asked. "She's old enough to marry if she pleases."

"She's always been such a sensible, respectful girl," Arabella went on, shaking her head. "I just can't believe that she's going to go through with it."

"I'm sorry about Kylie's involvement," Zach said. "I'm sure she doesn't mean to upset you. She's just got this thing about weddings."

Only when Arabella turned a wry, knowing look on him and Brooke cleared her throat did Zach realize what he'd just done. What gave him the right to apologize for Kylie?

"I'll admit that Kylie's involvement seems to have pushed things forward a bit," Arabella said, "but Jasmine and Cade were already engaged when she came into it. Can't blame her for that. What do you want to drink? Milk? Tea? Coffee?" She turned a smile on Zach. "Sorry, no cola."

Brooke opted for tea.

"Coffee," Zach decided. "I've only been out of bed for a little while. Maybe it'll help wake me up."

"How come? Busy night?" While Arabella poured herself a glass of milk, loaded a red enamel tray and carried it to the table, Zach explained about the burning tree.

Arabella clucked her tongue as she doled out beverages, small plates, forks and napkins. "Have you talked to Vincent?"

"I have. For all the good it did."

While Arabella transferred goodies onto small plates, Zach sipped from his cup of fragrant black coffee and reached for a bit of something that looked like a pinwheel of nut filling surrounded by dark cake. Popping the tidbit into his mouth, he hummed approval.

Arabella smiled and parked herself in a chair beside Brooke. "So this is your breakfast, huh?"

"Oh, no. Mrs. Jones made a breakfast fit for a king this morning, but that was about five."

Brooke laughed. "Lunch, then."

"More like pre-dinner dessert," Zach said, diving into the bounty with fork and fingers.

When he had knocked the edge off his hunger, he drew his phone from his pocket and placed it on the table. "I got a call from my buddy with the Florida state police. We need to talk about Lucas."

Sighing, Arabella sat back in her chair and crossed her legs. "I didn't think you came over for coffee cake and nut breads. What's going on?"

"We'll want to bring Mei and Vivienne in on this," Zach said before detailing what he'd learned. "Sis, will you call Viv? Arabella, if you'll speak to Mei, I'd appreciate it, but first, I think we ought to pray."

They all linked hands to pray before making their calls. After hearing what Zach had to say, Mei and Vivienne both concurred with the others that the time had come to bring in a private investigator. Zach picked up his own phone and began trying to get through to the person recommended to him. It took several minutes, but he finally got to speak to the P.I. Twenty minutes after that, the cousins and the investigator had comes to terms concerning his assignment via conference call.

"This may not work, but I really think it's the only thing we can do," Zach said after the call ended.

"I'm afraid you're right," Brooke agreed, "but at least it's something more than wringing our hands. That and prayer have been about our only options."

"Prayer is still our most powerful tool," Arabella pointed out.

"True," Brooke said.

Zach nodded. "I've certainly been praying more and more since I came back to Colorado."

"Is that good or bad?" Arabella asked wryly.

"Good," Zach replied. "It's good."

True, need or concern often spurred his prayers, but when in this life was that not an issue? Only in Heaven could one live free of need and fear. At least he had begun to regularly talk things over with God. Back in Miami, he'd let himself get into the habit of depending only on his own judgment and efforts. For a while, after the shooting, he hadn't been able to pray at all. Only after he'd let go of the guilt had he felt free to truly pray again. Kylie's confidence in him had given him the strength and surety for that.

Smiling, Brooke reached across the table to squeeze his hand. "Well, I, for one, am delighted to have you here."

"That makes two of us," Arabella told him.

Just then a little voice wailed, "Mama!"

Arabella popped up, calling out, "Coming!" She smiled apologetically at Zach and Brooke. "I'd better get to her before she wakes her sisters."

"I need to be going anyway," Brooke said, getting to her feet. "Gabe has some reports to go over this afternoon, so I'll be entertaining A.J."

Zach rose and they took their leave, thanking Arabella for her hospitality. As they passed by the living room, Zach stuck his head inside to speak to Kylie, only to find her missing.

"Oh, she had to get back to the diner," Jasmine said, thumbing through a magazine.

"Someone pick her up?"

"No, I don't think so."

That meant she would be walking. The diner was only a few blocks away, but Zach didn't like the idea of her being out on the street alone with Vincent doing his best to intimidate her. "Come on," he told Brooke, grabbing his hat on the way out of the house.

Fortunately, Kylie hadn't even made it to the end of the walkway. "Wait up," Zach called to her, fitting the hat onto his head.

She half-turned, but before either of them could speak, Arabella appeared with little Julie on her hip. The anxious expression on her face captured Zach's full attention.

"Something wrong?"

Arabella glanced at her daughter, saying, "I saw someone."

"What do you mean?"

Catching Brooke's eye, Arabella handed off the girl and pulled Zach toward the end of the porch where a double swing swayed gently in the breeze.

"I—I thought it was my imagination before, but I was raising the window in the bedroom just now and I saw him again."

"Saw who?"

"I don't know. A man. A strange man."

Zach pointed to the left, already moving in that direction. "Around here?"

"Yes. At the back of the house."

"Is the back door locked?"

"Yes."

"Stay here," he commanded.

He hopped over the railing so his footsteps on the planking of the wraparound porch would not give away his approach and ran around the corner of the house. Seeing nothing unusual, he swiftly checked the nooks and crannies before sliding around the next corner. Here the house cast a shadow, requiring Zach to poke through the shrubs.

He strode around to the front again, approaching from the opposite direction. Brooke and Arabella had joined Kylie at the edge of the street. Brooke still held Julie in her arms. Zach walked up to them and ruffled the girl's hair to lighten the mood. Smiling, she shyly hid her face in the crook of Brooke's neck.

"Anything?" Arabella asked.

Zach shook his head. "You've seen this person before, though, haven't you?"

"Yes. Twice before."

"And you're sure you don't know him?"

Arabella narrowed her eyes. "He does look familiar. He's not from around here, though, and I can't remember seeing him anywhere else." She shook her head. "No, I'd remember."

"Can you describe him?"

"Tall, even features, curly, dark blond hair. He's rather handsome, actually."

Zach patted Arabella's shoulder. "We should check the house."

She shook her head, saying softly, "I don't want to alarm the girls. Grandpa insisted we keep things locked up, so it's pretty much habit, but I've relaxed lately about the front door."

"Better start keeping that locked, too. Meanwhile, I'll feel better if we take a look inside. We can do it quietly. Come with me."

He had Brooke and Kylie wait outside with Julie, then walked into the house with Arabella. By unspoken agreement, they said nothing to Jasmine. Moving silently, they poked their heads into all the small spaces where an intruder might hide, but they found nothing. Every lower window and door proved to be locked, with the exception of the front door, as Arabella had said.

They went outside to find Brooke and Kylie enjoying the porch swing with Julie. Both women rose as Zach shook his head to let them know that no sign of an intruder had been found.

"Maybe I'm making too much of it," Arabella said.

Zach shook his head. "No…you're right to be cautious. If you see him again, you call me. Hear?"

"I will," she promised softly. The fear and concern in her brown-gold eyes stabbed straight into Zach's heart.

"I'll be keeping a watch," he promised.

She nodded and tried to smile. Zach patted her shoulder and watched as she said her goodbyes and shepherded little Julie into the house.

First Vincent and his mischief, and now a stranger lurking around a houseful of females? Who, Zach asked himself, was watching Arabella? And when did things around little Clayton, Colorado, get so complicated?

"Come on," Zach said, sliding his sunshades onto his face. "We'll give you a ride."

It wasn't exactly an invitation, but Kylie knew she could easily refuse. She swiftly considered doing so, but her desire to be with Zach—even if he did not seem particularly happy with her at the moment—overcame any minor trepidation. Besides, these things should be talked out. Although Brooke volunteered to get into the backseat of the uncovered Wrangler, Kylie insisted on doing so.

"In that case," Zach said, "I'll drop you off first, sis."

Kylie had allowed herself plenty of time to get back before the second half of her split shift began, but much of that time had been eaten up by the search for Arabella's trespasser. Still, she didn't object. From the moment of her arrival at the house, she had sensed Arabella's disapproval; now, she sensed Zach's. But surely they could agree to disagree on Jasmine and Cade's wedding plans? Neither of them could stop the young couple from getting married, after all. As they drove toward Bluebird Lane, she wondered how Brooke felt about the matter.

"I hope neither of you objects to my helping Jasmine plan the wedding."

Zach and his sister traded looks. Then Brooke sighed and shrugged. "I don't suppose it makes any difference one way or another."

Zach said nothing, but Kylie took heart from Brooke's answer. "The way I see it is that if they're determined to get married, at least they can have a nice ceremony and not go into debt for it."

Brooke nodded and relief flooded through Kylie. She bit her lip, her gaze on Zach. She couldn't see much more from this angle than hat and a glimpse of mirrored sunglasses, but she sensed his disapproval. "I hope that, if they do get married," she went on hesitantly, "you'll give Cade a chance. He really is a good kid."

"He's certainly been nothing but polite, kind and steady since I've been in Clayton," Brooke conceded, "and he's very faithful in church."

"I'm inclined to cut the kid a break myself," Zach said. "*Kid* being the operative word here, which is why I don't want them to get married."

"No one's saying they aren't young," Kylie pointed out, "but they are of legal age to marry."

Zach sighed. "Well, it's certainly not our call."

When he pulled up in front of Gabe's house, Brooke hopped out, waved and ran toward the front door. Kylie expected Zach to whip a U-turn and head downtown, but he just sat there for several seconds before reaching over and patting the seat next to him.

"What are you waiting for?" he asked. "Climb over."

"Oh." Kylie stood and carefully climbed over the seat. Sliding down into position, she reached for the safety belt. As soon as she buckled up, Zach hooked that U-turn and aimed the Jeep at downtown.

Kylie bucked up her courage and said, "I hope you aren't—"

"I'm not mad at you," he interrupted. "I'd prefer that you not help Jasmine plan this wedding, but I'm not angry. I'm troubled. I thought we were clear on that."

"I'm not sure you're clear on my position," Kylie ventured carefully. "I feel I must help Jasmine. I mean, if it were Mariette, God forbid, I'd help her."

"Even if your parents disapproved?"

"Yes, because they would understand why I was doing it. Offering support doesn't mean approval. It's just that if they're going to do this difficult thing, they're going to need all the support they can get."

Zach rubbed a hand across his nape. She'd noticed that he did that often, and it made her want to reach out and stroke him there. Remembering how he'd held her that morning while the tree burned and how safe and treasured he'd made her feel, she let herself do it. By the third time her fingertips brushed across his nape, he had relaxed his shoulders. When he nosed the vehicle into a parking space in front of the diner, her hand rested comfortably on the back of his neck. He killed the engine and leaned toward her, plucking the glasses from his face and folding them into his shirt pocket. His blue eyes held hers.

"Those kids are going to do what those kids are going to do," he said, sliding his arm across her shoulders. "I can't promise I can be as supportive as you are, but I am *not* angry with you about it. Or anything else. I don't think I could be angry with you even if I wanted to be, but if I ever *am* angry with you, you'll know it. Okay?"

"Okay."

He leaned toward her. She smiled softly, aware of her heartbeat accelerating as she waited for his kiss. Then the door to the diner slammed open, commanding their attention. Janey Guilder stumbled out of the diner. Rob Crenshaw careened along with her, grappling with her arm as she pumped it in an effort to avoid his grasp.

"Janey!" Kylie erupted, just as the other woman cried, "Let go of me!"

Without thinking, Kylie bailed out of the Jeep and ran to her friend. "Get away from her!"

"She comin' wi' me!" Rob yelled, spewing alcoholic fumes. He managed to get a grasp on Janey's arm and draw her back against him.

Kylie grabbed that hand and attempted to peel back his fingers. "She is not!"

"Let go!" Janey insisted, stumbling as Rob released her and shoved Kylie.

Reeling backward, Kylie managed to right herself as Rob yelled, "Stay out my bizniz!"

Suddenly, Zach had Rob facedown on the ground. He pressed a knee into the other man's back as he pulled a stiff vinyl strip from a pocket. As Zach bound Rob's hands with the plastic cuffs, Rob bucked ineffectually, bawling that he ought to break Kylie's nose for "stickin' it in my bizniz."

"You're under arrest," Zach said sternly, rattling off his rights, which Rob ignored.

"You 'zerve wha'er happens!" he snarled at Kylie. "You got 'tween me 'n my girl!"

"Hey," said an amused voice, "listen there. He's threatening Kylie."

She looked around to find that Vincent had stepped into the doorway. Zach sent him a glower. "Stay out of this, Vincent." Rising, he hauled Rob to his feet.

"You heard him!" Vincent insisted. "You accused me of terrorizing Kylie, but he's the one throwing around threats."

"Harassing," Zach corrected. "I *know* you've been harassing Kylie."

Vincent pointed at Rob. "How do you know it wasn't him?"

"She didn't break off her engagement to him on the day of the wedding," Zach snapped.

Vincent jerked his head at Kylie. "Maybe she was getting between Rob and Janey, like he said, leading him on maybe, busting them up."

"I did nothing of the sort!" Kylie protested. "You know I don't like drinkers! We argued about it often enough!"

"Then who is this secret admirer of yours?" Vincent sneered.

"I don't have a secret admirer, and you know it!"

"Ha! You're not the goody-two-shoes everyone thinks. You're with someone and you're ashamed of it!"

"I am not!" Kylie cried. She turned to Janey, pleading, "You don't believe that, do you?"

Before Janey could answer, Zach stated loudly, "Kylie has nothing to be ashamed of. I know that for a fact because *I* am the only one she's with. Kylie's *my* girl. No one else's."

For an instant, everything froze. Then Kylie's heart soared, pulling her up onto her toes. She half-fell, half-tiptoed past Rob and flung her arms around Zach's neck, knocking his hat askew. With one hand firmly clamped around Rob's biceps, Zach had only one arm with which to embrace her, but he set his hat straight and wrapped her tightly against his side, asking, "You got a problem with that, Vincent?"

"You're welcome to her," Vincent growled, then stalked off down the street in the general direction of the grocery store.

Erin replaced him in the doorway, grinning ear to ear. "Well, now that we've got that settled, are you coming in to work, or are you starting a new career as a necktie?"

Kylie spluttered, stuck somewhere between tears and laughter. "I'm coming." Yet, her arms remained locked around Zach's neck.

Chuckling, he patted her on the back. "Go on, darlin'. I have to get this knucklehead over to the county lockup. I'll be back later for dinner. Okay?"

"Okay," she squeaked, managing to loosen her hold enough to get her heels on the ground.

"Tell your dad I'll drive you home tonight," he added softly.

Nodding, she reluctantly dropped her arms. He smiled down at her, then turned to Janey. "I'll expect a full statement from you later. Understand?"

Hugging herself, Janey nodded. "Whatever you need."

"Good." Looking at Erin, he said, "Give her a cup of coffee or something, will you?"

"That's what we were doing when the boozehound there came in and tried to drag her out," Erin said, crooking her finger at Janey. Sliding behind Rob, who appeared to be befuddled, Janey followed Erin inside.

Zach pressed a kiss to the center of Kylie's forehead, tapped her on the nose with the tip of his finger and softly said, "See you later."

"Mmm-hmm."

He gave Rob a warning shake before pulling him along. Rob stumbled toward the Jeep, but Zach towed him across the street and then the greensward to put him into the caged backseat of the county sheriff's car. Kylie stood there watching them until Zach got in behind the steering wheel. Only then did she turn toward the diner, but she couldn't quite make herself go inside just yet. Everyone in the diner had no doubt heard what Zach had said. She wanted just a moment to hold the moment close before others started picking it apart with questions and innuendoes.

She laid her forehead against the doorjamb and relived the moment that he'd said, *Kylie's my girl.*

It was true, of course. She was Zach Clayton's girl. She had been for some time. She just hadn't been sure until that moment that he realized it!

Now everyone knew.

But what did that say about her dream to return to Denver and open her wedding planner business? She'd been willing to sacrifice that dream in order to liberate her family financially, but could she sacrifice it for Zach? He seemed firmly settled back in his hometown so could she be happy with him if he decided to stay in Clayton permanently?

But, could she be happy *without* Zach anywhere?

Obviously, she had some deep praying to do. She wanted to get it right this time. She had to know that Zach was the man God had chosen for her. Assuming, of course, that she was the woman God had set aside for Zach.

Oh, yes. Deep praying, indeed.

She couldn't yield her dream again for anything less than true love.

Chapter Thirteen

Erin kindly permitted Kylie to sit with Zach while he ate dinner that evening. It helped that he came in well after the dinner rush and that everyone who had been present during Rob Crenshaw's arrest had left the building hours earlier. The entire incident had undoubtedly been broadcast all over town by now, but to Kylie's surprise, Zach's announcement about the two of them had been met with a chorus of "duh," especially from her coworkers.

Apparently, their interest in each other had been obvious to one and all for some time. Kylie privately suspected that had set Vincent off and that he'd concocted this secret admirer nonsense in an effort to discourage Zach's interest in her. Fortunately, despite his long absence from Colorado, Zach knew Vincent well enough not to buy into his schemes. Yet, by silent mutual agreement, Kylie and Zach tiptoed around Zach's declaration, chatting instead about Rob.

"He was snoring by the time I got him to lockup," Zach revealed with a shake of his head. "Bet he's not sleeping so well now."

"How long do you think he'll be in jail?"

"Not long. Before he dropped off to sleep, he admitted to me that he'd been arrested before, but we didn't find any record of it. I suspect Diggers took him in hand a time or two, told him he was under arrest then let him go, so technically this is a first offense and as no serious harm was done, he'll get a slap on the wrist. I expect he'll spend tomorrow night at home, but at least he knows I mean business."

Kylie sighed. "I had hoped he'd be out of the way for a good while."

"I arrested him on charges of public drunkenness, assault and attempted abduction, but the DA will probably plead it down to the first count, and he'll get minimal bail. I just hope Janey isn't the one who posts his bond."

"I don't think she will be," Kylie said. "We had a bit of time to talk after you left. She's done."

"Good. That just means his father will bail him out, though."

She sighed impatiently. "Most likely."

"Well, not to worry. I know Rob's type. His courage is entirely liquid. I doubt Vincent could have instigated that scene if Rob hadn't been drunk already."

"So you believe Vincent is behind the whole thing?" she asked.

"Don't you?"

"Yeah. Yeah, I do."

"The way I see it, he was trying to cast suspicion on someone else," Zach said. "But I know too well how Vincent operates for that to work."

Kylie looked at him hopefully. "Maybe Rob will figure it out now."

"Wouldn't hold my breath until that happens." He wolfed down his dinner, then asked, "What's good for dessert?"

Erin told him that she had one piece of cherry pie left and a fresh quart of coconut pecan frozen yogurt.

He opted for the frozen yogurt, which won his instant approval. "This is delicious. Bet Macy would like this."

"You'll have to bring her in soon," Kylie said. "How's that Big Brother thing going, anyway?"

He made a face. "I've been too busy to spend time with her, but I'm not sure what to do with her anyway. It's not like Clayton is overflowing with entertainment venues."

"Well, there's the frozen yogurt," Kylie pointed out, "and I'm betting you could come up with something fun to do on the computer." She thought about it. "You could also ask around, see if you could find a horse for her to ride."

"That would be fun," he said. "I haven't ridden in years."

"You know what else you could do? A picnic."

"Now, that's an idea." He winked. "Thanks, darlin'. I'll give it some thought."

Kylie smiled. *Darlin'.* Was that going to be her special endearment? For as long as she could remember, her mom had been "sugar something-or-other" to her dad. Kylie and her sister had at times thought it funny. At other points, they'd considered it "gag worthy," as Mariette would put it. Ultimately, however, those little endearments had become as dear to them as they were to their mother. That constant evidence of their father's ardor for their mother both reassured and pleased them.

Suddenly, Kylie could imagine her own children reacting to their dad calling her "darlin'." She could see the giggles, the rolling eyes and finally the knowing smiles. Shaking herself out of the fantasy, she went to help close up the place.

Afterward, as Zach drove her home, he got a call from the sheriff's dispatcher. Someone had reported seeing a guy thrown from a car about ten miles east of Clayton. Zach dropped Kylie at her house and sped off to check it out.

Later, he called her to say that a young man from another town had gotten into an argument with his buddies as they drove toward some party. After they'd refused to turn around and take him home, he'd bailed out of the slowly moving car in a huff, tearing his shirt and skinning his chin. By the time Zach had gotten there, the kid had already called his mother to come and pick him up. Zach waited with him until she came.

Kylie marveled as they chatted about similar things that Zach had seen over the course of his career. Finally, Zach yawned and said he couldn't keep his eyes open any longer, so they got off the phone. Kylie lay in her bed, looking at the jagged shadow on the wall where once the moonlight had winked through the branches of the bigtooth maple outside. For the first time the room seemed utterly foreign to her, as if this was no longer quite her home.

When she thought of home now, she thought of the man who lay sleeping in a house on Bluebird Lane.

That notion compelled her to seek out Zach at church the next morning, and for the first time they wound up sitting together during the service. Afterward, Gabe and Brooke assumed that Kylie would join them and Zach for Sunday dinner. Zach, who appeared to be of the same mind, remarked that he'd give her a chance to change and pick her up later. Because the members of the Jones family usually fended for themselves on Sunday, Lynette being of the opinion that her single day of rest should be just that, Kylie readily went along with the plan.

She took it upon herself to contribute to the meal by preparing a colorful fruit salad. Seeing that, Zach swung by Arabella's for a bag of whole wheat rolls. She reported no further incidents at the house but had glimpsed the stranger more than once, always at a distance.

"Could just be someone new in town," Zach mused. "If I see anyone who fits the description, I'll speak to him, see what I can find out."

Arabella thanked him for that, then sighed. "Honestly, that's not the most disturbing thing that's happened lately.

My mother emailed to say that she might drop into town to say hello, if you can believe that."

"Kat?" Zach yelped, as if Arabella had another mother. His aunt had been absent from all their lives for so long that he couldn't help being surprised. "That is news." But what kind of news, he wondered, good or bad?

Arabella chuckled. "You sound just like Darlene. She was here helping to plan next quarter's kitchen schedule at the church when the email came. I think she was more rattled by the prospect of Mom showing up than I was."

Now why, Zach wondered, would Darlene care one way or another about Kat coming to town? Finding no easy answer, he mentally dropped the matter.

Arabella wouldn't take his money for the dinner rolls, so he paid her with a kiss on the cheek before heading back out to the Jeep and Kylie.

Brooke and Gabe welcomed their offerings with delight, and the two couples spent a comfortable afternoon together. Brooke seemed as surprised by Kat's suggestion that she might reappear in Clayton after all these years as Zach had been.

"Smelling money, maybe?" Gabe asked. Zach didn't want to say that or even think it, but it seemed logical. He changed the subject, and they talked about the possibility of arranging a horse riding lesson for Macy.

"Ask out at the Circle C," Brooke proposed.

They discussed getting a group together and making an afternoon of it, but before they could devise firm plans, Zach was called out to another auto accident.

"These mountain roads are treacherous," he muttered, preparing to leave.

"I'll say a prayer," Brooke volunteered, "and I'll take Kylie home, too."

"Thanks, sis," Zach said before looking to Kylie. "Sorry,

darlin'. I'll call you later if I'm not too late getting in. Otherwise, I'll see you tomorrow."

Nodding, Kylie turned her face up for his quick goodbye kiss. She didn't even think about it. Until she saw the knowing look on Brooke's face after he'd gone.

"Zach's girl," Brooke said around a grin, proving she'd heard the story.

Kylie wrinkled her nose. "Everyone's talking about that, are they?"

"Oh, yes."

"Does Zach know?" Kylie worried aloud, hoping he wouldn't mind being the subject of conversation.

"Oh yes. Know what he said when I asked him about it?"

"What?"

"He just looked at me, said, 'Duh,' and walked out of the room."

Laughter sputtered out of Kylie. Brooke didn't know why she laughed, and Kylie didn't attempt to explain. She delighted in knowing that Zach's sister apparently approved of their involvement. Conversely, the fact that Zach hadn't called by the time she turned in for the night did not thrill Kylie, but she assumed that he was working hard and that she could expect more of the same if they continued to see each other.

She did see him briefly at the diner the next morning, but he didn't have time to talk, not until mid-afternoon when he came in with Macy.

"Are we having frozen yogurt?" Kylie asked.

"We are," Zach confirmed. Macy asked for coins to put into the jukebox, and Zach handed them over. She ran off to pick her songs. He looked up at Kylie as she stood next to his chair. "Can you join us?"

She glanced around the busy room and made a face. "Best not."

"Give you a ride home later?"

"Yes, thank you."

"Let's hope no one else hits a heifer on the road," he muttered, obviously not wanting Macy to overhear.

"So that's what it was."

"Didn't help when the rancher showed up with a shotgun. Turned out he was worried he'd have to put the cow down, but it caused some consternation before it all got settled. The whole thing devolved into a shouting match between the driver of the car and the owner of the cow." Zach shook his head. "I felt like a nanny refereeing a pair of toddlers having a tantrum. Took half the night to resolve the thing, but the rancher shook my hand at the end and remarked that Diggers would've just gone home to bed and let them 'shoot it out.' I hope he was joking about that part."

"Not much," Macy piped up, proving that her ears were bigger than they'd assumed and her intellect a great deal sharper. She plopped back into her chair.

"Okay, my bad," Zach proclaimed. "No more talking shop with the munchkin in the room."

"I'm not a baby," Macy protested good-naturedly.

"True enough," Zach agreed, leaving it at that. "What kind of frozen yogurt do you want?"

Macy looked to Kylie. "What kind do you have?"

It wasn't a long list, only about half a dozen flavors. Most of the year, they only carried the standard vanilla and chocolate, but in the summertime Erin liked to offer a little more variety.

Macy made her choice without hesitation. "Coconut pecan!"

"Make that two," Zach said, grinning.

An elderly couple at the next table chuckled, leaned over and remarked, "Like daddy, like daughter, hmm?"

Kylie laughed, expecting Zach and Macy to join her. Instead, Zach looked as if he'd been poleaxed, and Macy's eyes actually filled with tears.

"I don't have a daddy," she whispered.

Zach cleared his throat and said, "I'm her Big Brother."

The couple took it literally.

"Well, no wonder you look so much alike."

"And have the same tastes."

Macy looked confused at that, but Zach's expression tuned positively grim. Kylie watched him forcibly lighten his own mood, the corners of his lips ratcheting up until he could wink at Macy and quip, "It's the rogue coconut pecan gene. Space aliens must've put it in the water." Macy giggled, and the awkward moment passed. "It's a plot to get us all addicted to coconuts and pecans," he elaborated.

"Because that's what they grow on their planet," Macy improvised.

They laughed over that bit of nonsense until Kylie went to dish up the goodies, but she knew that more was going on here than a shortsighted elderly couple making an erroneous assumption. Whatever it happened to be, she wanted to share it with him.

She wanted to share everything with Zach.

"I don't have a daddy," Zach repeated, shaking his head. He shifted on the porch step and smoothed a hand around the brim of the hat that he'd parked atop one knee. He'd decided that he needed a darker one for everyday and winter, but that could wait. Right now, he had Macy on his mind, Kylie at his side and a few things that he needed to talk through.

Kylie had turned out the porch lamps a few moments earlier so the mosquitoes wouldn't carry them away. He felt the big log house behind him, as solid as the ground on which it stood.

"It was heartbreaking when Macy said that," Kylie agreed,

leaning against him. "I never really thought about how it must be for her. I can't imagine what my life would have been like without my dad."

Zach sighed, guilt weighing on him, and confessed, "I never got along with my father."

"You mentioned that before," Kylie said, snuggling a little closer. "What was the problem?" He felt her shiver and lifted an arm to loop it about her. The nighttime temperature routinely dropped to below sixty degrees in July, sometimes well below.

"Cold?"

"Not now," she told him, laying her head on his shoulder and warming his heart. "Are you avoiding my question?"

He briefly considered avoiding *that* question, but he knew how he'd feel if the shoe were on the other foot, so to speak. He wanted perfect honesty from her, so he had to give her perfect honesty. He did not want to face his own culpability in his relationship with his father, but he couldn't avoid that. Not anymore. Not after today.

"I don't want to talk about my dad and me," he said.

"Okay then."

"I don't want to," he went on, "but I need to."

She turned her face up to him, her cheek nesting in the hollow of his shoulder. "I'm listening."

Zach gazed off into the darkness. The quiet out here on Waxwing Road felt absolute. Clayton and the rest of the world might as well not exist. He looked up at the sky. Millions of stars twinkled against the deep blackness of space. Yet, he did not feel small and insignificant; he felt as if God looked down upon him, as if God targeted him with His complete, patient, loving regard. Zach understood fully in that moment that he had more than one father—and that he still had a chance to be a good son.

He began to tell Kylie how like his grandfather his father

had been. As he spoke, Zach recalled all the criticism of his grandfather that he'd heard from Samuel's side of the family and even, on occasion, from his own mother. He could understand her problems with George Sr., but he saw now that he had let that criticism of his grandfather, whether just or not, color his image of his dad.

"I was too ready to take issue," Zach decided, "too quick to judge. Dad was busy, but we might have spent more time together if I'd occasionally cut him a break. He was just a man, after all, like any other, but I expected him to be more than he could be. And he had his own problems with my grandfather." Zach shook his head. "I cheated myself out of the close relationship with my dad that I actually wanted. I suspect that he did the same with my grandfather. I'm more like him than I knew."

"Then he must have been a better man than you know," Kylie said softly, sliding her arms around him.

Zach smiled, but so many thoughts clogged his mind that he barely heard her. How far did it go? he wondered. Had George Sr.'s judgments of Great-Grandpa Jim added distance to their relationship? If so, could that cycle be stopped? He had to believe that it could be, with honesty, realization and, most of all, God's guidance.

Kylie offered no further comment. She didn't argue or rationalize. She just held him while he spun apart. He hoped that when he came back together again, he would like what he had become. But would Kylie? More importantly, would God?

Father, he prayed silently, *help me be all that You would have me be. Help me be a better man and Christian than I was a son. Help me be what Macy needs to fill that hole in her heart.*

Suddenly he remembered what that elderly couple in the diner had said about how alike he and Macy were in appearance. He'd noticed her similarity to his sisters, but he'd never thought about any likeness that he might share with her. He remembered another incident, too.

"You know," he said abruptly, "tonight wasn't the first time I've been told that Macy and I bear a resemblance."

Kylie lifted her head. "Really?"

He nodded. "The other day I ran into Macy and Darlene in the grocery store, and another woman walked by. I know her, but I'm not sure she recognized me. She's five or six years older than me. Anyway, she stopped to talk to Darlene, but when she first walked up she said, 'Boy, do you two look alike.' I thought she meant Darlene and Macy, but she was smiling at me when she said it, and now that I think about it, Darlene and Macy don't resemble each other all that much, do they?"

Kylie tilted her head as if picturing the pair in her mind's eye. "No. They don't. Although Macy does seem to have Darlene's nose."

"But Macy and I do," he stated.

Wide-eyed, Kylie studied him. "It's the Clayton dimple. And the shape of your faces." She blinked, adding, "And the way your mouth moves sometimes."

She stared off into space for a several moments, and then she asked, "Do you think Macy's father might be a Clayton?"

"Yeah." Zach nodded. "I do. In fact, I think it's likely."

"But who could it be?" she asked.

"I see plenty of possibilities," he told her, arching an eyebrow. "Don't you?"

"Yes." She looked down at her knees, then said, "I don't like gossip, but I've heard some speculation about how Darlene couldn't afford her house and why she came here to Clayton to live. It all makes sense if one of the Claytons is Macy's father and he paid her off to keep quiet about it."

"Unfortunately, for much of my family that idea is not outside the realm of possibility."

"Doesn't paint a very pretty picture of Darlene, though, does it?" Kylie said sadly.

Zach shrugged. "How many women do you know who trusted the wrong man?"

"True. And I have to admit that Darlene is a wonderful mother. She would do anything for Macy, including keeping her mouth shut in order to put a roof over her head."

"That must be why Darlene asked Brooke and Gabe to raise Macy when she can no longer care for the girl herself," Zach surmised.

"And you to be her Big Brother," Kylie pointed out. "Perhaps she's trying to give Macy her real family or as much of it as she can."

Zach closed his eyes, refusing to think why she might have singled out him and Brooke from all the other Claytons. It might be simply that she had access to and liked them. He certainly wouldn't have entrusted a child to Vincent or his sister Marsha, not to mention Pauley and Charley, and Cade was too young. Zach thought of Jack McCord, Cade's half-brother. Could Macy be Cade's half-sister? Zach identified some similarities between the two, but then he shook his head.

He couldn't solve this mystery with the information that he had, and what difference did it make anyway? He'd committed himself to Macy, and even if she didn't turn out to be family, he'd live up to that commitment.

"I've been thinking about that picnic you mentioned," he said to Kylie.

She smiled. "Yeah?"

Looking down at her, he smiled. "I don't suppose you have any time off this week, do you?"

Her own smile grew. "I might."

"I think I'm due some time off myself," Zach told her. "How does Thursday sound?"

"I'll check with the sheriff and Darlene and let you know."

Kylie rubbed her hands together. "I wonder what we should have to eat."

Zach chuckled. "I'll leave that up to you."

"Okay, but you have to pick the spot."

"Deal."

"Any place in mind?"

He smiled and said mysteriously, "Maybe."

He did have a place in mind, actually, but he wanted to surprise her with it, see what she thought about it. Besides, he wanted to do some scouting around, be sure that his memory hadn't played him false. It had been a long time since he'd been out that way.

She laughed. "In that case, you can just wait and see what you get for your picnic lunch. We are talking lunch, aren't we?"

"I imagine so."

"Hmm," Kylie said, narrowing her eyes, "I may have to talk to Arabella and Erin."

"Oh, yes," he encouraged heartily. "Do that."

Kylie laughed again. "I have to talk to them for Jasmine anyway."

Zach felt his smile fade, but he snuggled Kylie to his side and let it all just...go. He let go of a lot while sitting there over the next hour or so on that porch step with Kylie. He let go of his resentment toward his late father, and while he was at it, he let go of his resentment toward his grandfather, too. He even released his stubborn hold on the last vestiges of his grief for all those whose deaths had touched him so deeply: Lucy, his mom, his dad, his grandpa, even his grandmother, long ago. And Dave. For the first time, the possibility of seeing his friend and family members in Heaven seemed real to Zach, and he allowed himself to take comfort in that.

Looking up at the sky again, he felt as if he saw everything with fresh eyes, as if the world—his world—had begun anew.

Chapter Fourteen

The land sloped gently from a partially bald rise set against the mountain and fringed on three sides with a mixture of trees. Zach recognized juniper and spruce, white fir, maples and birch. Less conversant with the types of wildflowers, he couldn't name them, but he certainly appreciated the vibrant, crazy-quilt beauty that blanketed the slope right to the edge of the narrow, stony brook bubbling down from the mountains. The flowers gave way to green where the brook dwindled to a trickle that disappeared into a tiny crevice folded into the gray-brown rocks, only to break from the flat, grassy ground further down in a gurgling gush at the edge of a small pond.

The spot was even more beautiful than he remembered. Easy access along a gentle ridge and sufficient soil made the bald knob of the rise a perfect site for a house, and he could see with his mind's eye a sprawling log edifice with a big stone chimney and deep porches there. The pond would freeze in winter, providing a perfect skating surface, and he could almost hear the laughter of children as their sleds zipped down the snow-covered slope.

In a perfect world, he would choose to build a home and raise a family right here in this spot. He wondered if Kylie would like it, or if her determination to return to Denver would blind her to the beauty of this place.

Turning, he looked across the valley floor to the Jones homestead. The house itself appeared no larger than his thumbnail at this distance, which meant that this place stood well outside the environs of Clayton. He wondered how Kylie would feel about that. He felt increasingly desperate to change her mind about Denver. Working his jaw from side to side, he pondered her desire to open a bridal shop and become a full-time wedding consultant. Was it even fair of him to ask her to give that up? Could he find a way to be happy in Denver or another large city again?

"Borrowing trouble," he told himself.

She hadn't even brought it up in a while. Besides, no one but God knew what would happen. For one thing, with Lucas out of pocket, Samuel could inherit all, including the very ground upon which Zach now stood. For another, he had no real idea what Kylie might be thinking about the future. He knew that she felt as drawn to him as he did to her and that she cared for him, but he doubted that she could be thinking about marriage mere weeks after essentially leaving Vincent at the altar. He could hardly believe that *he* was thinking about it. But he was, of course, even if he had just admitted it to himself. Borrowing trouble, indeed!

Turing off the thought, he tilted his head back to gaze up at the wide, pale blue bowl of the sky. A dirty cloud poised over the tip of a mountain, casting the deep shadow that signaled rain. At that altitude, some snow remained year round. The cold, icy rain would create real danger for anyone up there. If the cloud moved in this direction before it had dumped its load, their picnic could be washed out. Zach didn't think it would be a problem, but the sooner they got to it, the more time they'd have to enjoy themselves. He checked his watch. His half-day off had started ten minutes ago.

He climbed into the Jeep and lit out. When he arrived at his place, Darlene and Macy sat in front of the house in Darlene's old rattletrap car. Zach pulled up in his usual spot, deeming it more reasonable to go through the house than stop in the street to greet them and then get back into the Jeep to park. He used his key to let himself in the mudroom door and rushed into the kitchen, nearly mowing down Kylie.

"Oh! Hi," she said, laughing. "I let myself in like you told me to."

At the same time, he said, "Oops. Macy's out front. I need to get out there."

"Go," she said, even as he strode toward the front of the house. Her laughter followed him through the house and kept a smile on his face as he exited onto the porch. Swiftly crossing that, he jogged lightly down the steps and along the walk. Darlene and Macy met him halfway.

Macy hugged him warmly and could barely contain her excitement. "Oh, I love picnics! Picnics and tea parties, but picnics have better food. What are we having?"

Zach chuckled, caught up in her youthful exuberance. After all the hardship with her mother, Macy deserved to have some fun. "Kylie's in charge of the food. Go on inside and see what she's got for us, if you want."

Macy ran for the house. Zach and Darlene both laughed, watching her go.

"Want to sit for a minute?" he asked Darlene, gesturing toward the porch.

She slowly ambled in that direction, saying, "I can't tell you how much this means to Macy. Or to me."

"Aw, it's my pleasure," Zach said. "She's a sweet kid. Good fun."

Darlene acknowledged the compliment with a smile. "Thank you. I think she's special, of course."

"She is special."

Darlene bowed her head, saying, "You may know something about my health issues."

Zach nodded. "Brooke told me."

"I assumed she would, given our…arrangement."

Zach recognized an opening when he saw one, and he took it. "I know you said Macy's father couldn't help, but don't you think, for her sake, that we ought to know his name?" Darlene immediately began shaking her head, but Zach pressed on. "Just from a health history standpoint, it would be helpful, and she's going to want to know one day. You know she is."

Darlene bit her lip. Just then, Kylie and Macy clattered out of the house and onto the porch.

"Zach," Macy called, "I'd like the lemonade, pleeease. Mama won't let me have soft drinks."

"And your mom's wise not to let you have them," Zach said, winking at Darlene. "Those things are addictive. I'm living proof of that."

"Just want to be sure that the lemonade in the fridge isn't Brooke's," Kylie said. "I mean, we all *know* what you drink."

"The lemonade could be A.J.'s," Darlene put in.

Zach grimaced. "You're right. I'd better run next door to ask." Brooke would be watching A.J. while Gabe worked, but she and the boy went back and forth all the time. She could well have gotten the lemonade for him. Zach looked at Kylie. "Just let me change first, okay?" He patted the holstered gun on his hip. "A.J. is already curious about this holster. I'd prefer to keep it out of his sight as much as possible."

He could phone, but if the boy wasn't up from his morning nap and the call woke him, Brooke would have Zach's head on a platter. His baby sister had become a regular mama bear, and it pleased Zach to no end. Besides, he needed to change before they headed off on their picnic anyway.

"I'll get out of your way," Darlene said, moving back down

the walkway toward her car. "Bye, honey," she called to her daughter. "Have fun."

"I will, Mama." Macy produced a fashion doll and went to the corner of the porch, behind the half-wall, where she fell to her knees. The doll appeared on the top of the half-wall. As she skipped it toward a big pot of flowers in the center of the ledge, she sang, "We're going on a picnic. We're going on a picnic."

Zach and Kylie shared a smile as he hurried into the house with long, rapid strides.

"Is there a blanket we can use?" she asked as he moved past her.

"Sure. The linen closet's in the laundry room. Check there."

Leaving Macy on the front porch to play, he pointed Kylie toward the laundry room and went into the bedroom to change. As usual, he hung his hat on the edge of the mirror, stashed his badge and gun in the dresser drawer then stripped off his uniform shirt and went to the closet to pull a soft chambray shirt from its hanger. He slung it on and began doing up the snaps, freezing as he heard a scream and then a crash coming from the front porch.

Macy! He ran out of the room, sure that she had somehow knocked the big flowerpot off the half-wall. Kylie was already going through the front door.

"Macy? Are you hurt?"

Zach darted around Kylie and went to the girl, confused by what he saw. The pot lay shattered, not on the ground but on the porch. Had she somehow *pulled it off* the top of the half-wall?

Kylie moved forward to run her hands over Macy, starting at the top of the girl's head and sliding over her shoulders and down her arms. "Are you okay? Did you hurt yourself?"

Trembling, Macy pointed a finger at the wall.

"H-he pushed it!"

"What?" Kylie looked to the smashed flowerpot.

Zach bent over the girl. "What did you say?"

She turned huge, frightened eyes up at him. "That man. He whispered, 'Watch out!' Then he pushed the flowerpot."

Zach went cold. "What man?"

Macy shook her head and pointed around the corner of the house. "I don't know. He went that way."

It made no sense, but Zach wasn't taking any chances. He ran, but no sooner had he rounded the corner than he realized that he was unarmed. Back into the house he went and straight to the bedroom dresser. When he saw that the drawer stood open and empty, he froze. Gone! His service revolver and badge were gone!

The flowerpot had been a distraction. He realized suddenly that he hadn't even closed the drawer when he'd stowed his gun. Normally, he'd have done so before leaving the room, but this time he hadn't.

Once again, he'd allowed himself to be disarmed! What kind of lawman did that?

He wrenched the drawer free and threw it across the room. Then he dove over the bed for the backup sidearm that he kept in the bedside table. Tucking it into the waistband of his jeans, he rushed back out onto the porch.

Striding toward the steps, he barked at Kylie, "Call Darlene. Now! When she gets here, I want the two of you to go with her."

"Where are you going?" Kylie demanded, racing to the edge of the porch.

"After whoever did this!"

He slid around the corner of the house, paused and took stock, one hand gripping the butt of his gun. If Vincent had pulled this stunt, he'd have cut across the backyard, circled around Gabe's place and crossed the little field on the other side to his own place. Zach doubted that Vincent would risk having this traced back to him, but it had to be checked out.

Moving swiftly, Zach covered the ground in just a few minutes and beat a fist on Vincent's back door. Receiving no answer, he went around to the front. The drive was empty, and no one answered his attempt to get into the house. By all appearances, Vincent was not at home, and Zach had no legal authority to force his way inside.

Frustrated, he jogged back up the road, seeing Darlene's car once again driving away from his house and toward downtown. As he turned up the walkway, Kylie moved into view on the porch.

"I thought I told you to go with Darlene."

"Don't do that, Zach."

He threw out his arm, striding toward the Jeep. "What?"

"Treat me like I'm just another citizen."

He stopped, his heart pounding, and turned on her. "I don't want you in danger."

"There isn't any danger," she said calmly, coming down the steps and toward him.

"He took my badge and gun!" Zach shouted.

"Ah," Kylie said.

"I let it happen again!" Zach raged on. "I let down my guard. I let myself be disarmed!"

"You did not," Kylie interrupted. "This was planned to embarrass you."

Zach stared at her, his hands clamped against the nape of his neck. She was right, of course. He'd already realized that the flowerpot had been used as a distraction. Kylie came to him and wrapped a hand around his biceps.

"Don't you see? Whoever did this knows about what happened in Miami. This isn't just about us. It's not just about me. This is about *you*."

Zach shook his head, so much whirling through his mind.

"Think!" Kylie urged. "If someone wanted to steal your gun and badge, where would they look? If it were me, I would assume that you'd keep them close to you, and I'd watch for a moment when you were distracted to try to steal them."

He'd given the thief the perfect opportunity. He'd as good as announced that he'd be leaving the gun in the house while he talked to Brooke. Then he didn't even close the drawer! He'd once thought that he was a good cop. Then he'd let that druggie in Miami lay hands on his gun, and Dave had died. Nothing had been right since. He'd lost it. Whatever he'd had, whatever had made him an effective lawman, he'd lost it.

"I can't do this job anymore," he said. "I can't do this job."

Kylie shook his arm. "Don't say that! Can't you see that he wants to rob you? He wants to rob you of your inheritance. Of your self-confidence. Of your *calling*."

Zach stared down at her. "Vincent."

"Yes. But that's not who Macy saw."

Zach dropped his hands to her shoulders. "Macy knows who broke the flowerpot?"

Kylie shook her head, "No. But I know who she saw. At least, I know who she described." He tightened his grip on her arms. "His name's Willy Bishop."

Willy Bishop. The sniveling little creep who'd framed Zach for theft back in high school. "We go way back, Willy and I. He's an old friend of Vincent's."

"And he shares a house with Rob Crenshaw."

Zach reared his head, those law enforcement instincts roaring back to life. Of course. Vincent had set this up. Just as he'd goaded Rob into making that scene at the Cowboy Café, he had surely arranged this. That first little scheme had almost backfired, though. Vincent must have been appalled to find that Kylie wasn't at the café when Rob had first accosted Janey. Well, this wouldn't work, either, not with Willy Bishop as Vincent's tool.

"Stay here," he said to Kylie, setting her aside, but he didn't manage a single step before she came back at him.

"No."

"Kylie…" he began impatiently.

"No! I have to prove to him—and to you—that there is one thing he cannot take from you no matter what he does," she said fiercely, "because *I* won't let him!" She wrapped her arms around Zach, almost like the day they'd met, the day she'd called off the wedding and run from the church, the day he'd first stood between her and Vincent. Except this time she faced him, so he could read those beautiful eyes. "He can't take *me* away from you, Zach, because I won't allow it."

Stunned, Zach felt his heart rate speed up. "Kylie?"

"The rest is all up to you," she told him, "but I won't let him, or anyone else, decide who I love. Not even you. That's for me to decide. That's between me and God."

"Kylie!" His lungs pumping like a bellows, he locked her against him, whispering, "Kylie." He could scarcely believe what he'd heard. Had he even heard what he thought he had? Could she, *did* she, love him?

He must've hugged her so tightly that she couldn't breathe for she made a sound partway between a laugh and a gurgle as she pushed against him. Instantly, he released her. She danced away, moving toward the Jeep.

"Well, come on," she said. "Let's go get him."

Zach smiled, feeling invigorated, confident, strong. "You don't need to be involved in this," he told her, striding once more toward the Wrangler.

"Yes, I do," she insisted, going to the passenger door. "Willy's a slimy little weasel. He's probably gone to ground by now, but I know all his hidey holes."

Zach grinned. Well, she had him there. Besides, from what he had learned about Willy, Zach had to rate the likelihood of danger at practically nil. On top of that, he didn't really want to let her out of his sight. Ever again. He got into the Jeep. She sat belted in place before he got the engine started. Still shaking his head, he backed the Wrangler up the drive and out into the street.

"I trust you know where this house is that Rob Crenshaw shares with Willy."

"It just so happens that I do."

"Point the way, darlin'."

But then, hadn't she already done so? In more ways than she could possibly know.

The house on Flicker Avenue had little to recommend it. In need of paint and shingles, it might once have been a snug little cottage, but rusted car parts, including an engine and one entire front end of an ancient pickup truck, littered the dusty front yard. The shrubs flanking the open gateway of a nonexistent fence and lining the front of the house had been allowed to grow unchecked, blocking windows and shooting off unruly sprouts in all directions. The first time she'd come here, Kylie had wondered if the place was even occupied.

"Wait here," Zach said, climbing out of the Jeep.

Kylie just looked at him. Really? He thought that would work *now?* She knew Willy, and although he might have considered it a lark to steal Zach's service revolver and badge and stood in awe of Vincent, Willy wasn't the sort to actually brandish a weapon or strike a blow. A soft, sleazy character with teeth like a rat's, Willy kept to the back of every crowd and slinked around the perimeter of every room. He'd scare a little girl, yes, and do Vincent's dirty work if it didn't prove too difficult, but he'd fold like a card table if confronted. Vincent could move him to tears with a single look. Kylie could just imagine what Zach could do.

She slipped out of the vehicle but hung back while Zach knocked, bouncing the screen in its frame. Opening the screen, he looked through the tiny window set high in the cracked wood of the front door. Growling with frustration, he pounded harder.

"Crenshaw! Rob Crenshaw! I know you're in there!"

Rolling her eyes, Kylie rushed forward and slipped around Zach to open the door.

"What are you doing?" he hissed. "I can't—"

"I can," she interrupted. "I'm not the law, and I've done this more than once when I was looking for Vincent."

He lifted his eyebrows, inclining his head. She turned the knob and pushed the unlocked door open, calling out, "Willy? Rob?"

A snuffle, not unlike that of a pig going after an acorn, drew her attention to the tattered recliner in front of the bulky TV to one side of the dim, dirty room. Rob shifted and sighed, obviously sinking back into a deep sleep. Kylie walked over and shook him by the shoulder, shouting, "Rob!"

He jerked and tried to bolt up, but the chair itself hampered him. He did manage to get the footrest down. Scruffy and rumpled, he squinted up at her. "Kylie?"

"Yeah. We're looking for Willy. Do you know where he is?"

Shaking his head, Rob glanced around at the lumpy, dirty, grey sofa, yellowed lamp shade, gouged side tables and worn, oversize easy chair spilling its stuffing from one arm. "He, uh, he was here when I passed ou—uh, went to sleep."

"And when was that?" Zach asked from the doorway.

Rob's eyes widened as he took in the big man silhouetted there. "Uh, uh, about dawn, I guess."

Zach nodded, asking, "Mind if I take a look around?"

Rob blinked and licked his lips. "What for?"

"I think Willy paid me a visit a little while ago," Zach said, every word weighted with portent.

Rob's eyes again tracked warily around the room.

Kylie tried for a friendly tone, asking, "You don't want to be in the way of an investigation, do you, Rob?"

"Obstructing," Zach corrected. "The charge is obstructing an official investigation."

"I'm not obstructing anything!" Rob exclaimed. "You can't arrest me again! I'm not drunk and I'm not obstructing!"

"Great. Guess that means I can take a look around then," Zach said, sauntering into the room. "Thanks, Rob."

Gulping, Rob wiped a hand over his face. Kylie felt kind of sorry for him and patted his shoulder. Zach stood in the center of the floor, his arms at his waist, carefully surveying the room. He presented, she noticed, a quite imposing figure, and it came to him as naturally as breathing.

Couldn't do this job! She mentally scoffed at the very idea. He'd been born for this job, made for it. And she had been made for him. She didn't doubt it now, only feared that, in the end, he wouldn't see it. He hadn't, after all, told her that he loved her—and God knew she'd left that door wide open.

"How many rooms do you have here?" Zach asked.

"F-four. Uh, not counting the bathroom."

"Well, it wouldn't be in his room. Even Willy is too smart for that."

"What?" Rob squawked. "What?"

Ignoring him, Zach tilted his head. His focus lasered in on the sofa. "Does that look unusually lumpy to you?"

Kylie studied the section of the sofa in which he seemed interested. It did look oddly shaped. He went over and flipped back the cushion. She knew from the way his shoulders relaxed that he'd found what he'd been looking for. Trust Willy to pick the most obvious hiding place. Bending, Zach picked up the missing items and turned to face Rob.

Kylie thought, for a moment, that Rob would choke. Then she wondered if he would manage to climb the recliner backward.

"I—I've never seen that before! I don't know anything

about it! I don't know how it got here!" All but bawling, he grabbed Kylie's hand as if to plead for her protection.

"Oh, for goodness sake," she said, "just tell him what he wants to know."

The corner of Zach's lip quirked, but he managed to keep a straight face. "Who was here last night?"

Rob rattled off several names, starting with Willy.

"And Vincent?"

Rob gulped and confirmed sulkily, "Yes, Vincent." He quickly added, "Vincent's a friend of Willy's."

"But not yours?" Zach asked.

"Not anymore," Rob muttered.

"That's smart, Rob. That's real smart. See, Vincent uses people, like he used you that day I had to arrest you. Right?"

Rob began to look hunted, but he clamped his lips firmly shut.

Zach frowned. "So, did you at any time overhear Vincent and Willy discussing a theft?"

Rob shook his head wildly. "No. No, no, no."

"A prank, maybe, that they wanted to play on me?" Zach suggested.

Rob insisted brusquely, "I didn't hear what they were saying. Okay? I didn't want to hear."

Kylie watched Zach slide the badge into his pocket and check the holstered gun. Apparently resigned to the fact that Vincent was going to get away with another stunt, he strolled toward Rob. Bending at the waist, he trapped Rob in the chair, his hands planted on the recliner's arms. One of them held the gun snapped into its holster.

"Where is Willy?"

Staring at that covered holster, Rob cleared his throat. "He said he was going to see his aunt. Told me I could rent out his room."

"What's her name?"

Rob screwed up his face. "Uh…Jenny? Betty? Something like that."

Zach hung his head, communicating his displeasure. "Where does she live?"

"Texas," Rob said. "Definitely Texas."

Sighing, Zach straightened. "Show me his room."

Rob managed to get to his feet, and the two of them disappeared through a doorway. Zach returned alone a few minutes later.

"Well, old Willy definitely packed up and lit out. I think Rob's just now coming to grips with the idea that Willy and Vincent might have been setting him up. Wouldn't be the first time those two framed an innocent man."

"Are you going after Willy or having him picked up?"

Zach shook his head. "If I could, I'd apologize to Texas, though."

Kylie chuckled and let him steer her out of the house. He stopped in front of the Jeep and put back his head, heaving a great sigh of relief.

"You okay?" Kylie asked.

He turned to face her, leaning a hip against the fender. "Better than okay."

"No more doubts about the job?"

He looked down at his booted toes. After a moment, he shook his head. "No more doubts about the job."

"Thank God!"

"Thank God," he echoed. "And you."

"Oh, I didn't do anything," she said. "Not really." Then, before he could argue the point, she asked, "What now?"

"First," he said, holding the holstered gun aloft, "I lock this away." He went to fiddle around with the backseat, flipping it up. A metal box had been fixed to the floorboard. He opened it, put the gun inside, locked it and repositioned the seat.

"Let's grab a bite to eat," he suggested. "Then I'll call Macy and reschedule our picnic. Looks like it's going to rain anyway."

Kylie turned her face up. "So it does."

"Better get the top on first. Want to help me? Again."

She grinned. "Absolutely." *Always,* she added silently.

He went to the back of the vehicle and took out the vinyl top. Working together, they had the thing snapped into place within minutes. Obviously, they made a good team.

"Just in time," Zach said as the first drops started to fall. They hopped in.

"So, you want to go back to your place and picnic indoors?" Kylie asked, thinking of the food she'd left in his refrigerator.

He looked at her and smiled, then shook his head. "I don't think being alone with you right now is a good idea." He started up the Jeep and threw the transmission into gear. "Not a good idea at all."

She blinked at him, confused and a little hurt. Did he fear that she'd press him for a declaration now that she'd let him know how she felt?

Maybe his silence on the subject was his declaration. Maybe he just didn't feel for her what she felt for him. Sure, he'd publicly claimed her as his girl, but that could have been just to thwart Vincent. Later, he had to know that it had gotten all over town, hence his remark to Brooke on the subject. Besides, tagging her as his "girl" fell far short of entertaining thoughts of marriage, and she admitted to herself that she wanted to be his wife. True love, yes, that had to be part of it, but being Zach's girl would never be enough for her. She wanted to spend the rest of her life with this incredible man. But maybe he never would want to marry her.

That thought saddened Kylie. It threatened to break her

heart. But if she'd learned anything, she had learned to wait on God, to let Him reveal His will in His time.

She had tried before to shape His will to suit her idea of what was best. She had intended to marry a man she did not love for what she now realized were, ultimately, selfish reasons. Thankfully, God had not let her get away with it!

If she now loved a man who did not feel for her what she desperately wanted him to feel, well, she supposed some poetic justice could be found in that. It would break her heart if Zach did not eventually come to love her, but God would see her through. She would not doubt that He had a reason, a plan. She would embrace His plan—even if it came with pain—and in the meantime, she would pray as she had never before prayed.

Chapter Fifteen

~⟋~

They went to the Cowboy Café. Kylie tried not to be disappointed. Where else, after all, could they go to get a meal?

Darlene and Macy had apparently come up with the same idea and were already sitting at a table. Macy waved at them over a dish of coconut pecan frozen yogurt, the last of it, probably, unless Erin had purchased more of the stuff. If Erin hadn't, Kylie mused, she might pick up some of Zach's favorite frozen yogurt herself.

Darlene got up from the table and came to meet them, asking softly, "Everything okay? What exactly happened?"

Zach gave her an expurgated account. "It was a prank of sorts. I don't think any harm was meant toward Macy. Otherwise, he wouldn't have given warning before shoving the flowerpot off the porch ledge." He exhaled sharply. "At any rate, we know who did it, and he's apparently left town. If he shows his face around here any time soon, though, I'll be all over him."

Darlene nodded. "Want to join us? We're almost done, actually, but Macy will feel better if she gets to spend a little time with you."

Kylie and Zach followed Darlene to the table. She looked more frail all the time. Macy smiled pensively and, glancing out the window, commented, "Guess this wasn't the day for a picnic, huh?"

"We'll do it another day," Zach promised, helping Kylie into her chair. He sat next to Macy and explained that she had nothing to fear from the "prankster" who had pushed over the flowerpot.

"It just all got me by surprise," she said, looking a little embarrassed. "I didn't know he was even there until he said to look out. That's what surprised me and made me scream like that."

"You were right to scream," Zach told her. "Don't worry about him. He won't be pulling any more stunts like that around here anytime soon. It turns out that he's decided to visit family in another state."

Macy shrugged and polished off the frozen yogurt. They sat around talking while Zach and Kylie decided what to eat. The downpour passed. Darlene shepherded Macy out the door, saying that she had to get back to her job at the church.

Kylie turned in their order and carried drinks to the table—iced tea for her, the usual soft drink for Zach. Their food came mere minutes later, and Zach tucked in with his customary gusto. Kylie slowly put away her sandwich and fruit salad while Zach demolished his double cheeseburger and a mountain of french fries then drained his drink. She got up to fetch him another. When she returned, she saw that he had spread his hands across the tabletop, thumbs and fore-fingers meeting to create a triangle.

As Kylie sat down again he said, "My grandma used to say that the triangle represented God's completeness, Father, Son, Spirit in One. When I'd misbehave, she'd lift her hands and peer at me through the triangle that she made with her fingers." He demonstrated, lifting his hands to his face so that the triangle formed by his fingers framed his eye. "That was her way of reminding me that God was watching."

"Excellent imagery."

He nodded. "I guess I forgot that God is always watching me. He doesn't just know what I'm doing at any given moment, though. He's always aware of everything that goes on in my life and all that I need. I have to trust Him to be there, guiding me, in every situation and to provide my needs. I can't depend just on myself." He met her eyes. "I see now that I was depending on me alone. I guess I had to come back here to Clayton in order to remember that God is watching."

"I understand," Kylie told him.

He smiled. "I know you do."

"Makes me think of Clayton in a whole new way, though," she murmured. "Clayton was a trap to me."

"Was?"

She nodded, then hastened back to the real subject. "I think you're telling me that Vincent can't win because God will deal with him. The law may constrain your actions, but we can depend on God for justice and protection."

"That pretty much sums it up," Zach said. "We both know that Vincent put Willy up to this latest stunt, but we're never going to prove it. Willy took the rap for him before. He'd do it again. I have to accept that and leave Vincent to God."

"So even though Vincent may think he's gotten away again, it's only temporary."

"Until God's purpose is achieved," Zach expounded, nodding. "And I firmly believe there is a purpose. No matter what hateful thing Vincent does next, God will use it for His own reasons."

Kylie lifted her hands, touching forefinger to forefinger and thumb to thumb. She looked through the resulting triangle. "God is watching."

"All of us," Zach added. "Vincent included."

She sipped iced tea, thinking. "How do you suppose Vincent found out about what happened in Miami?"

Zach shrugged. "All he would need is a connection to the internet. It was all over the papers down there."

"That's true. So he found it and he tried to figure out a way to use it to crush you."

Nodding, Zach said, "He might have succeeded if not for you." He held up his thumb and forefinger, leaving only the tiniest space between them. "I was this close to walking away from the job."

"I don't believe that," she scoffed. "You're not a quitter. If you were, you'd have quit after Miami. You had much more reason then."

"Maybe."

"No 'maybe' about it. Besides, your sisters and cousins are depending on you."

"I didn't say I would leave Clayton," he began, but before he could expound on that thought, a group of young people poured through the door, laughing and talking. Kylie instantly identified her sister, along with Jasmine and Cade.

"Picnic got rained out, huh?" Mariette surmised, coming to stand beside Kylie while the other kids pulled two tables together and rearranged chairs.

"Something like that. What's up with you guys?"

"Oh, things are slow at the store, and Cade got off early because of the rain, so a bunch of us decided to get some sodas and hang out for a little while."

"I see."

Mariette smiled and went to claim a seat at the table with her friends. A moment later, Jasmine and Cade strolled over. Smiling at Kylie, Jasmine pulled out the chair on Zach's left and dropped down onto it, while Cade remained standing behind her.

"We want to talk to you about something," Jasmine said, looking at Zach. "We can wait and stop by your office, if you want."

Zach spread his hands. "No point in waiting. What's on your mind?"

Cade placed a hand on Jasmine's shoulder. She smiled and leaned both forearms on the tabletop. "We been thinking about it and…I'd really like you to walk me down the aisle."

The look on Zach's face would have been comical if Jasmine's hadn't been so earnest.

"Me?" he choked out after a moment, thumping himself in the chest. "You want *me* to walk you down the aisle?"

"You're, like, the family protector," Jasmine said. "Well, the community protector, really. And since my dad's no longer in my life…" She shrugged, adding dryly, "He never was in my life, really. Not in a long time, anyway. Not since he started drinking. And you're someone I admire. You're what I wish my dad could be. I just hoped… Will you at least consider it?"

Kylie held her breath, her heart going out to both of them. She hated to see Zach put on the spot like this, but who else could Jasmine ask? The pastor would be performing the ceremony, after all, and Cade's half-brother Jack was against the marriage. Besides, none of the men on Cade's side of the family could compare with Zach. The protector.

That, she realized, was his role. He was not just the avenger of injustices or the enforcer of the law, though both would naturally play into his true purpose—protecting the weak and needy. But would Zach see this request of Jasmine's as falling too far outside his normal role?

She watched as he slumped back in his chair and thought it over. After a moment, he shifted his gaze to Cade.

"Are you in agreement on this?"

Cade did not hesitate. "I am. You're Arabella's family, and she's the closest thing to family that Jasmine has. Besides, Jasmine respects you. We both do."

Zach lifted a hand to the back of his neck and cleared his

throat. "I still think you're too young to get married," he said. Jasmine wilted and Cade squeezed her shoulder. "But you're obviously two bright, mature, responsible individuals," Zach went on, leaning forward again, "and you're obviously in love. So, if and when the day comes that the two of you marry, I'd be honored to walk you down the aisle, Jasmine."

Cade let out a relieved breath, but Kylie would have missed it if she hadn't been glancing at him when Jasmine shrieked with glee. Launching herself across the corner of the table, Jasmine threw her arms around Zach's neck and hugged him.

"Thank you! Thank you, thank you, thank you!" She dropped back into the chair. "You don't know how much this means to me." Suddenly she popped up to her feet. "I have to tell Arabella!" Turning to those at her table, she called out, "Guys! I have to run home. Wait for me. I won't be long."

She rushed out. Cade stayed behind for a moment. Turning to Zach, he put out his hand.

"Thank you." After only a slight hesitation, Zach put his hand in Cade's, and they shook. "I know you aren't convinced that getting married is the right thing for us to do," Cade told him, "but I'll always be grateful to you for making her so happy just now." With that, he turned and followed her out the door at a trot.

Zach sighed, groaning, "Oh, man. Arabella's going to think I've given this wedding my blessing."

"Haven't you?" Kylie asked, unable to hide her smile.

He screwed up his face. "Kinda, sorta, maybe." Watching through the window as Cade caught up to Jasmine on the far side of the green, he added, "I have to give it to that kid. He wants Jasmine to be happy."

"You think so?"

"More than anything in the world."

"He loves her," Kylie said softly.

Zach's gaze switched to her face. "Yeah," he admitted. "He does. I see that now."

Kylie nodded. "Is that why you did it? Why you agreed?"

"Partly," Zach answered. "That and what she said about her dad not being in her life. My dad was there, and I wasted that. *We* wasted that, both of us. Jasmine hasn't been as blessed as I was, and she deserves someone who cares to walk her up that aisle, no matter when the wedding takes place. I couldn't refuse."

Kylie laid a hand on his forearm where it rested on the table. "You are a good man, Zach Clayton. Jasmine chose wisely."

He gave her a lopsided smile. "I hope you mean that."

"Of course, I do."

He dug into his pocket and pulled out several dollar bills. Tossing them onto the table, he said, "Let's get out of here. I want to show you something."

Kylie rose as he did and began gathering up the dishes. "Okay. Just let me bus this table."

"Leave it," Zach said. "It's your day off."

She blinked at him in surprise, but she'd already stacked the dishes. "Won't take a minute."

He nodded, so she quickly carried the dishes behind the counter and dumped them into the big plastic tub there. One of the other waitresses said she'd wipe the table, so Kylie left it at that, but just as she reached Zach, Mariette skipped over, asking, "Hey, guys, can I get a ride out to the house? Dad's sweeping out the storage bins and I don't want to bother him, but I promised someone we'd chat online this afternoon, and my laptop's at home."

Kylie looked at Zach, who seemed to gnash his teeth, but then he smiled tautly and nodded. "Sure. We're heading out that way. We'll drop you."

"Great! Thanks." She waved to her friends and bounced out of the building.

Kylie telegraphed her thanks with a look and smile, wondering what Zach wanted to show her. Somehow, from his tone, she'd gotten the idea that it had to do with his past, something else that bound him to Clayton perhaps. She realized then that she, too, was bound to Clayton. By him. By the possibility that they might, one day, have a future together. It seemed that she had yielded her dream after all. She had traded it for another.

They dropped Mariette off at the Jones place.

"Does she ever just walk?" Zach asked, watching the girl skip and twirl toward the house.

"Not so you'd notice." Chuckling, Kylie lifted her long hair and pulled it over one shoulder. The cover on the Jeep made it stuffy and warm inside, and she fanned herself with her hand. "Where to now?"

"It's not far," Zach hedged, trying to keep his tone light. He switched on the air conditioning, pretending that he wasn't more nervous than he'd ever been in his life.

He wondered if he'd lost his mind. The urgent need to do this had seized him back there in the diner, but he'd started to doubt. Was God derailing him? Had he misread Kylie's words and actions? Maybe he should forget the whole thing. But he wouldn't. He couldn't.

He turned right onto Waxwing Road and headed away from town. When he came to the trail, he judged the mud as nothing that his vehicle couldn't handle. The wildflowers on the slope appeared less lush than they had before the rainstorm, but the brook burbled happily, the water like crystal. He brought the Wrangler to a halt at the top of the knob.

"This is it."

Kylie looked around her then glanced at him before

opening the door of the vehicle and gingerly stepping down onto the ground. Choosing her steps carefully, she made her way to the front of the Jeep and turned a slow circle.

Lord, give me the words, Zach prayed silently before joining her.

"Where are we?" she asked.

He pointed to the log home in the distance. "That's your parents' place there."

She flashed him a look. "I know that. I mean, what piece of property is this?"

"Ah. It belonged to my grandfather. I used to ride my bike out here or get one of my parents to drop me off. Sometimes I'd bring a friend. We'd fish in the pond at the bottom of the hill, play war in the woods, go sledding and ice skating in the winter. We even camped out up here a few times."

"And this was going to be our picnic spot today, wasn't it?" she surmised. He nodded. "It's beautiful," she said, lifting her arms as if to bask in the beauty around them.

"I'd like to build a house here someday," he confessed in a rush. "I don't know that I'll ever be able to. The property could wind up being Samuel's someday. I think he's counting on it, in fact, and that's probably why he got your father to help him buy the property between this section and your folks' place."

She blinked at that. "He thought Dad would default on the loan and he'd get it all, didn't he?"

"Maybe."

She folded her arms. "That's not going to happen. We're keeping the payments current, and you and your sister are doing your part to fulfill the terms of your grandfather's will. Surely your other sister and cousins will do the same."

"I don't know," Zach said. "We can't find Lucas, and I'm not entirely sure that Vivienne will make it. I think she will. I know she'll try, anyway."

Kylie shook her head. "Doesn't matter," she said. "Samuel can plot and plan, but he can't compete with God. Somehow, it's all going to work out. I'm sure of it. You'll build your house here."

"Will you live here with me?" Zach heard himself ask. At the stunned expression on her face, he muttered, "That didn't come out right."

At the same time she asked, "What did you say?"

Zach tried to hear his own thoughts over the pounding of his heart. "I know you aren't keen on the idea of staying in Clayton. I just thought that if maybe I could show you the possibilities for the future, you'd…" He stopped and cleared his throat, rethinking. "I don't want this to be a deal breaker, though."

"What deal?"

He shook his head, trying desperately to finish his thought. "I mean, you could run your wedding business online. Granted, I don't know beans about that stuff, but you could consult and advise, locate resources, even offer designs and recipes, whatever. They even have that video conferencing thing."

"I've thought about it," she said off-handedly. "But what deal? You said that you don't want this place to be a deal breaker. I want to know what deal you're talking about!"

Zach opened his mouth and what came out was "I love you."

As if her bones had turned to water, she wilted against the bumper of the Wrangler. He reached toward her, afraid she'd wind up on the ground in a puddle, but she stiffened and barked, "Well, why didn't you say so?"

"Uh…"

"Why didn't you say it when I did?"

He opened his mouth, closed it again, blew out his breath. "I, um, I guess I thought I'd already made it clear."

He frowned, remembering. "And you didn't exactly say it, either."

"I didn't?"

"No."

She narrowed her eyes. "I thought I did."

He tilted his head, feeling a smile budding deep inside his chest. "Come on," he said, gesturing with both hands. "Give."

She lifted her chin, parked her hands on her hips and tilted forward slightly. "I. Love. You."

It was all he could do to contain that smile. It felt, in fact, as if it might burst from his chest, but one or two items remained. "What about Denver?"

"What about it?"

"We can go there if you want," he said, stepping closer. "Once I've done my part to meet the stipulations of my grandfather's will."

"Why would *we* go anywhere together?" she prodded, inching forward.

"Because," he told her, sliding his arms around her and pulling her close, "that's what married people do. They go places together. They live together."

"In that case," she whispered, "together is all I care about. Where doesn't matter."

He closed his eyes. "Did you just agree to marry me?"

"Yes, I believe I did."

He huffed out a sharp breath. "Thank God," he said, then, "I love you. I really love you."

She wrapped her arms around his waist. "I love you, too."

"And no matter what happens," he promised, smiling down into her face, "we'll have a place to live. I can talk to my sisters about us taking over my mom's house. I mean, Brooke's going to move in with Gabe when they marry, and I can't see Vivienne staying more than her year if she even makes it back for that."

"I don't care where we live," Kylie told him, propping her chin on his chest. "We could move in with my folks if it comes to that."

"About your folks," Zach began, reeling out his thoughts. "I have some money put back, and I ought to be able to stash a good bit more cash because I'm not even paying rent now, so even if I don't inherit that quarter million from my grandpa, I can help them retire that debt."

Kylie straightened, and tears filled her eyes. "You'd do that for us?"

"For you," he said softly. "I'd do it for you."

She gasped and lifted trembling fingers to cover her trembling lips. "You really are the finest man!" she squeaked.

"No," he said. "I just love you."

She slid her arms around him, squeezing. Hard. He laughed, joy welling inside him.

"So," he teased, "while you're planning all these weddings, will you plan one for us?"

He felt her smile. "Honestly, I've been doing that for a while now. In my dreams."

His own smile stretched so wide that he thought his face might split. Holding her close, he felt the pieces of his life settle into place.

It seemed wise, given that she'd run away from a wedding slightly less than a month earlier, that they bide their time, but neither wanted to wait too long.

"Maybe we should talk it over with your parents," Zach suggested. "See what they think. Will they be shocked?"

She thought about it and shook her head. "No. I think they'll be pleased but not really surprised. Vincent, though…"

"Leave him to God," Zach said. "Just leave him to God."

He had learned to leave much to God because God never failed. He always had a reason and a plan. Others could try to muck up God's plans or shape them to fit their own, but God always made a way to bring His children home. Even when they didn't know where to find home. Even when home was the last place they ever expected it to be.

Turning her face up with a finger beneath her chin, Zach kissed his future wife, thankful that God hadn't left him alone in Miami. He belonged in Clayton. They both belonged in Clayton. Together.

* * * * *

Dear Reader,

Have you ever convinced yourself that you have correctly discerned God's will, only to realize that you've let your emotions lead you to an erroneous conclusion? Too often our emotions get in the way of our faith. We hurt, so we think that God is punishing us. We fear, so we assume that God has abandoned us. We tire, so we worry that God has forgotten us. We covet, so we feel that God doesn't care about us.

Sometimes, hanging in and keeping on are more difficult for Christians than anything else, because we don't trust God to have our best interests at heart. As our heroine, Kylie, finds out, however, God will often rescue us even from ourselves—if we let Him.

Do you need to be rescued from yourself? Remember that sometimes all God requires of us is that we hang in and keep on.

God bless.

Arlene James

Questions for Discussion

1. Kylie Jones had convinced herself that she had correctly interpreted God's will, only to find that she had been led astray by her own emotions. Has this ever happened to you? Why do you think we are sometimes led astray by our emotions?

2. Sometimes Christians who suffer trauma blame God. Zach Clayton suffered the trauma of witnessing the death of his partner and blamed himself. Is it better to blame one's self rather than God? Why or why not?

3. Kylie convinced herself that marriage to Vincent Clayton was God's solution to her problems. Can you point to any examples in the Bible where God allowed His children to provide their own solutions? What happened? (See Genesis 16–17, 29–30 and Matthew 26:14; 27:1–6.)

4. A favorite old saying is: "I complained because I had no shoes until I met a man who had no feet." How does this apply to Macy, who never knew her father, and to Zach?

5. Zach resented his late grandfather's influence over his father, only to realize much later that he had allowed his resentment to stunt his relationship with his dad. Can you identify such pointless resentments in your own life?

6. Can you identify such pointless resentments in the Bible? (See Genesis 37; Matthew 26:6–12.)

7. Zach never expected to return to his hometown, but when circumstances conspired against him, he found

himself right back where he'd started. Can you remember a time in your life when circumstances conspired against you? Did you identify this as God's hand at work in your life?

8. Can you think of a Bible story when God used circumstances to force someone's hand? (See the Book of Jonah.) What might Zach have done to spare himself the circumstances that brought him back to Clayton? What might any of us do to spare ourselves the discomfort of unwelcome circumstances in our lives?

9. Psalm 12, verse 5 reads: "Because of the oppression of the weak and the groaning of the needy, I will now arise," says the Lord. "I will protect them from those who malign them." Peace officers are expected to protect the weak and oppressed, but they are constrained by a complicated set of rules and rulings. This frustrated both Zach and Kylie. Did God, nevertheless, protect Kylie and her family from those who would malign them? How? Did God protect Zach, too?

10. Zach's first encounter with Rob Crenshaw came at the community-wide Independence Day picnic. Zach's solution at that time was to approach an angry, inebriated, verbally abusive Rob with a handshake and a soft word. Why did this work? Does God ever approach us in the same way? If so, how might that happen? (See Matthew 15:15–18.)

11. Zach's second encounter with Rob Crenshaw came at the Cowboy Café. At that time, Zach swiftly used force to subdue Crenshaw. Why? Was this a correct approach? Why or why not?

12. Vincent sought to undermine Zach by having a cohort steal Zach's gun and badge. Why do you think Vincent chose this particular action?

13. Evil seeks to use our vulnerabilities against us. What is Christ's approach to our individual vulnerabilities? (See Luke 19:1–10.)

14. Kylie set aside her dream of becoming a wedding planner when she became engaged to Vincent. After refusing to marry Vincent, she reclaimed her dream, only to relinquish it again when she fell in love with Zach. What does this say about Kylie's dream?

15. As Christians, should we allow ourselves to have dreams or ambitions? Why or why not? Is it possible that God gives us dreams but we are mistaken about how they are meant to play out? (See Genesis 29:16–28.)

INSPIRATIONAL

Inspirational romances to warm your heart & soul.

Love Inspired.

TITLES AVAILABLE NEXT MONTH

Available August 30, 2011

HER RODEO COWBOY
Mule Hollow Homecoming
Debra Clopton

THE DOCTOR'S FAMILY
Rocky Mountain Heirs
Lenora Worth

THE RANCHER'S RETURN
Home to Hartley Creek
Carolyne Aarsen

A FAMILY OF THEIR OWN
Dreams Come True
Gail Gaymer Martin

SAFE IN HIS ARMS
Dana Corbit

MENDED HEARTS
Men of Allegany County
Ruth Logan Herne

LICNM0811

REQUEST YOUR FREE BOOKS!

2 FREE INSPIRATIONAL NOVELS
PLUS 2
FREE
MYSTERY GIFTS

Love Inspired

*When private eye Skylar Grady is kidnapped and
abandoned in the Arizona desert, she knows her
investigation has someone scared enough to kill.
Tracker Jonas Sampson finds her—but can he keep her
safe? Read on for a sneak preview of LONE DEFENDER
by Shirlee McCoy, from her HEROES FOR HIRE series.*

"The storm isn't the only thing I'm worried about." He
didn't slow, and she had no choice but to try to keep up.

"What do you mean?"

"I've seen camp fires the past couple of nights. You said
someone drove you out here and left you—"

"I'm not just saying it. It happened."

"A person who goes to that kind of effort probably isn't
going to sit around hoping that you're dead."

"You think a killer is on our trail?"

"I think there's a possibility. Conserve your energy. You
may need it before the night is over."

"I still think—"

"Shh." He slid his palm up her arm, the warning in his
touch doing more than words to keep her silent. She waited,
ears straining for some sign that they weren't alone.

Nothing but dead quiet, and a stillness that filled Skylar
with dread.

A soft click broke the silence.

She was on the ground before she could think, Jonas
right beside her.

She turned her head, met his eyes.

"That was a gun safety."

He pressed a finger to her lips, pulled something from
beneath his jacket.

A Glock.

They weren't completely helpless, then.

He wasn't, at least.

She felt a second of relief, and then Jonas was gone, and she was alone again.

Alone, cowering on the desert floor, waiting to be picked off by an assassin's bullet.

No way. There was absolutely no way she was going to die without a fight.

A soft shuffle came from her left, and she stilled as a shadow crept toward her. She launched herself toward him, realizing her weakness as she barreled into the man's chest, bounced backward, landed hard. She barely managed to dive to the left as the man aimed a pistol, pulled the trigger. The bullet slammed into the ground a foot from where she'd been, and she was up again.

Fight or die.

It was as simple as that.

*Don't miss LONE DEFENDER by Shirlee McCoy,
available September 2011 from Love Inspired Suspense.*

Love Inspired

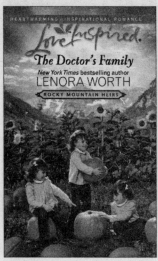

Raising four-year-old triplets and an abandoned teenager, single mom Arabella Clayton Michaels loves her big family. But when Denver surgeon Jonathan Turner arrives to announce that Arabella's beloved teenager is his long-lost niece, they find themselves becoming an unexpected family....

The Doctor's Family

By *New York Times* bestselling author

Lenora Worth

◆ ROCKY MOUNTAIN HEIRS ◆

Available September wherever books are sold.

www.LoveInspiredBooks.com

LI87692